Game For Fame

by

Y'vet

Game For Fame

To Bert, Richard and Mommie. I love you.

Chapter 1

"Ow!" Chandelle screamed trying desperately to make some room between the iron and the skin around her wrists. "You have the right to remain silent. Anything you say may be held against you in a court of law..." Chandelle faintly heard the towering officer. Retracing her memory she pondered where the plan went wrong; A month of planning and covering each detail... *How the hell could something so right go so wrong?*

"Ma'm! Ma'm! Do you understand your rights as they were just explained to you?" Chandelle's only response was a nod, yes, as she sat, her mind still in a fog. Pittsburgh's finest interrupted her thoughts, "You are being arrested for murder in the first degree, possession of a fire arm, and anything else the DA comes up with when he gets a hold of your case."

"Chandelle! Get your ass down here now! Every time we want to go out we're always waiting on your ass! It's late. There's nothing you can do to fix that ugly mug of yours. And I still have to pick up Rachel and Nia! So hurry up! Damn!" Rena yelled.

"I'm coming. Just go out to the car. I'll be there in a minute!" *See that's why I hate going out with these crows. Always acting like they missing something. Same ole shit. Ain't nothing going on we haven't already done or invented ourselves. Same tired clubs and equally broke men profilin' in them. Rushing out there for nothin'. I don't have any money to be trying to hang every weekend in the first place. They know it's the first of the month and the rent is due.*

Chandelle took one more glimpse in the hallway mirror checking out her reflection from every angle making sure everything was in its proper place. She took great pride in her appearance. At five foot eight and a hundred and forty pounds with legs for days, Chandelle was blessed with the looks many a thirty-five year old woman would die for. She carried her weight well with thick hips, buttocks and thighs with a tight waist mirroring the taut stomach of a twenty year old. Sporting a shoulder length wrap with brown hues, it complimented her honey brown complexion nicely. Nodding with approval she blew a kiss at her reflection and walked down the stairs locking the door behind her.

"Rena tell me something. Do you think you have that music loud enough? This ain't the damn ghetto and my neighbors are not having that loud shit at all hours of the night." Chandelle leaned over turning down Whodini talking bout the freaks come out at night. "Girl I don't know where your mind is at. But I know you're up to no good listening to the freaks come out at night. You need to keep that mess to yourself when you're riding solo. What do I look like pulling up to the club with that song blasting from the speakers? I ain't a freak and I don't give my goodies away to no freeloading anybody who thinks he can get it."

"See Chandelle why do you have to go there? Why can't I just listen to Whodini because I was reminiscing about when this song came out? Remember the eighth grade school picnic at Kennywood? Remember when we met that fine ass Jeffrey and his boys by the Jack Rabbit. Hmmph! That's when life was good and living was easy."

"See, that's what I'm talking about. It always involves some guy. Remember what happened at the end of the night when our asses got stranded out near Homestead? And what were we doing? Following behind some trflin' niggas tryna go to some party we knew nothing about and their cheap asses didn't even have enough money to get us home. Then they had the nerve to ask us to meet them downtown the next day. Those were the days.

I remember my mother whoopin' my ass and fussing about picking us up in the middle of nowhere and as if that wasn't enough she put me on punishment for a week after that. Here I am twenty-five years later doing the same ol' shit. You better be glad I love your ass!" Chandelle said laughing.

Chandelle and Rena had been best friends since kindergarten when the first day of school each gravitated toward the other. Ms. Roth the kindergarten teacher lined up her new students in a single filed line, Rena standing in front of Chandelle. Rena turned around in line noticing Chandelle's shoes and spoke first.

"I like your shoes. They're cute. Where your moms shop for your clothes?" Rena looked Chandelle up and down appreciating her outfit. Rena continued,

"My mom takes me to Sears. She loves Sears. She always says they have guarantees on everything. Our whole house is Sears. They come to your house and fix anything broken if you have the warranty. I tried to tell mommy they wasn't coming to see about my ugly clothes. Hate 'em. It's all white girl stuff and it lasts forever. Never could wear them out or nothing so I can get something new." Ms. Roth asked that they quiet down so Chandelle never had a chance to answer. Rena never gave anyone a chance to say much about anything.

"Where are we going anyway? What's the plan this time?"

Rena slowed down at the light anticipating whether she wanted to make a right and go the shortcut risking running into her ex she knew was posting up on the corner or take the left and be fifteen minutes later than they already were. Running into Ricky was a nightmare she didn't feel like dealing with right now. She knew he would flag her down and she would be inclined to stop because she needed his readily available bankroll. Making the right won out. She'd sweet talk her way through this dilemma as she has many times before.

"Well, we're going to ride by, scoop up Rachel then Nia and head out to the *River's Edge*." Rena stated matter-of-factly.

"For what?!!! I told you when you called me earlier at work that I needed to pay my rent. I can't afford the casino tonight. You might as well turn around and take my ass home right now!!! "Chandelle was fuming.

"Chill girl! I got you. I'm going to pay the cover so you can get into the club. You don't have to gamble. We're going to check out the house band scheduled to play tonight. Heard they were the bomb. I'm even going to front you your first two drinks. You have enough shit going on with you to have some man feeling sorry for you and buy drinks the rest of the night. Who knows you may get lucky. Hell, I don't know why you don't get over what happened between you and Derek. There are other brothas out there girl. You just won't chill long enough to find out. Let Derek ruin the rest of your life if you want to but I'll be damned if I let a man dictate mine. Anyway, just try to have a good time Chandelle. Don't mess it up for everybody." Rena looked over at Chandelle who was looking out the window appearing as if she hadn't heard a word she said. Rena knew better though. They were like sisters and she knew Chandelle heard every word.

Rena pulled up to Rachel's complex and rolled down the window, "What's up girl? You ain't on time are you?" Rena and Chandelle started laughing. "Not anxious to get your groove on are you? "

"Ha! Ha! Ya'll can't be on time for your own funerals. You know we are running late. I was just trying to be ready so we can find a parking space and catch the first act" Rachel smiled and rolled her eyes.

"Get in cow!! You ain't foolin' nobody! You know your hot ass is just trying to get first dibs on the goodies!" They all broke out in laughter. "Rachel what do you have on? Your outfit sure doesn't leave much to the imagination." Chandelle asked while peering at her friend from the front seat of the car. Rachel was always the wild one in the bunch from her flamboyant personality to her taste in fashions. Rachel wasn't drop dead gorgeous but was always able to stop traffic. She didn't have the beauty of a runway model but her shapely figure and attitude always commanded attention and wherever she went there was always an attentive audience.

"This little number is called the Man Slayer. I won't be surprised if I'm married with two kids by next year with this outfit." Rachel laughed as she picked an imaginary piece of thread from the front of her dress as she crossed her legs exposing the deep split up the left side of her thigh.

"It's *what* you're going to be married to you better worry about. You'll mess around and your new *husband* will be pimpin' your ass on Liberty by the bus depot." Chandelle cracked.

"See Chandelle your wrong! Rena laughed. "You know you're wrong don't you?"

"Don't say nothin' to her Rena. Chandelle can only pray to look this good. She could try to have a little bit more style and take lessons and maybe she would have a life other than watching reruns of The Jefferson's and chowin' down on Orville Redenbacher and diet Pepsi every night." Rachel ignored Chandelle and made an attempt to change the subject.

"Anybody call Nia? I didn't bring a bottle and I don't see one. I hope she ran by the liquor store to pick one up. I want a couple of drinks before we hit the club. I'm tired of spending my money on them high ass drinks and not feelin' nothin'. Don't make no sense how much they want for a Remy and Coke these days."

"I hear you. I was just telling Rena on the way over here that I didn't have any money for the *Rivers Edge* tonight. I can't afford to do it like I would like to either. I am so tired of talking about how broke I am all the time. We need to find a way to get a hustle of our own so that we can live the way four divas are supposed to live." High fives were given all around.

7

Game For Fame

Rena and Chandelle met Nia during their senior year in high school through Tyrik a member of the crew. Tyrik got together with Nia at the annual senior class hooky picnic. It was the event of the year when the seniors across the city would meet at Schenley Park to drink and barbeque. The friends frequently cut classes together going to different city high schools drinking and being disruptive. Tyrik dated Nia the following three years after graduation and married a year after that. They remained close ever since.

"Chandelle we are pulling up to Nia's. Run out and ring her doorbell. Don't go in. Just tell her we're here and hurry up so we can get to the club." Chandelle opened the door and walked up the pathway to let Nia know they were waiting and ready.

Chapter 2

"Damn! Did the honies show up tonight or what? Ladies check out table number one on the left by the fireplace. Is he my babies' daddy or what?" Rachel's tongue was hanging on the floor making a spectacle of herself as usual.

"Can't go nowhere with ya'll. Just don't know how to act! Rachel breathe easy. C'mon let's go find a seat at the bar. Maybe I can save face and act like I'm not with you. Embarrassing me out here like y'all ain't ever had a man in your life!" Chandelle walked towards the bar trying to picking up her pace as if she wasn't with the three women still staring at the brotha at the table.

"Rena what's up with your girl? She sure has been acting funny lately. If she wasn't my girl I'd swear she couldn't appreciate a fine specimen of a man like that one over there. She can act stupid if she wants to but I get mine." Rachel glanced backwards to make sure handsome was still alone and available.

"She'll be okay. She just hasn't gotten over Derek yet. He really did a number on her. I don't know how long it's going to take her to get over it. But we're her girls and we owe it to her to stand behind her while she goes through this. Rachel, order yourself a drink on me and go get your man." Rachel approached the bar and ordered a drink and made her way to the unsuspecting gentleman across the room.

"Rena where are you getting all this cash? You're really showing some love tonight aren't you?" Nia asked curiously.

9

Game For Fame

"I got a couple of dollars but you know I'm deep in Ricky's pockets. I'm going to ride that horse 'til it dries up. We have an agreement. He takes care of my bills and wardrobe and I take care of him. You know what I mean?"

Nia looked at Rena in amazement. "So you're telling me that you are hoeing yourself out now? Is it that bad girl? You know that you don't give a shit about him. He's ain't about nothing. Besides, he's a drug dealer. What the hell are you thinking? You're going to find yourself caught up. Dead, jail, or even worse, your mama is going to find out. I'm serious. How many stories have you heard about these wanna be drug dealers stashing stuff in their women's houses and then when they get caught they want to say it's not theirs to keep their asses out of jail. Guess who does the time? It's not worth it girl. Get out now while you still can. I know it's hard right now and Tyrik and I have problems too. I'm trying to hold my own thing down right through here and it's rough for all of us right now but all in all you have a decent life. Your place is gorgeous and you have a nine to five that pays enough to keep your bills straight." Nia stated deeply concerned.

"I hear you girl. I was thinking about him and our *agreement* earlier. I'm just trying to dump his behind with as little bruising as possible. The last time I tried to cut it off he followed me around for a week until I promised to take him back. He was so cute then whining and begging that I didn't have the heart to let him go. *It didn't hurt that Ricky has the striking resemblance of Idris Elba. Fine can hardly describe how good that man looks.* Still, Ricky just wants that trophy girlfriend he can showcase in front of his friends. He's always bragging that he has the finest woman in the 'Burgh. It's my 38D's, chocolate thighs and stylish flare that keeps him interested. We have nothing in common but the love for the almighty dollar. But now it's old, my biological clocks ticking and I'm looking for the real deal. He has to go. I just have to figure out when and how. But enough about me is there something I can do to help you concerning your marriage?"

"No. But thanks girl. I can handle Tyrik. I just want you to be careful whatever you decide to do. You know you can call me when you need me. If you like I can have Tyrik talk to him." Nia took a sip of her drink and waited for Rena to reply.

"Nia I love you but you know I would never bring you and your husband into my mess. I'll take care of it. And trust me I'll let you know when the dirty deed is done so you won't have to worry." Rena leaned over and hugged Nia.

"I only pray that one day I'll have what you and Tyrik have. You know you're my shero." Rena said sincerely.

"Stop with the sentimental bullshit Rena. I'm not trying to start crying in here. We're here to get our party on. Order another drink and let's get over there and rescue Chandelle. She looks as though she's being molested at the bar.

"Chandelle! Introduce us to your friend." Rena said looking at the burly man with the crooked teeth standing in front of her.

"Ladies, this is um…um what did you say your name was again?" Chandelle watched her new acquaintance smile revealing a gold tooth up front and center while missing his entire bottom row. Nia and Rena backed up when they were attacked by his breath that smelled like the bottom of a sewer.

"Jacob. Pleased to meet you. Damn ladies! The two of you are as fine as your friend here. This must be my lucky day! I was just trying to convince your friend here to come out on the dance floor and show me what she's working with. Maybe one of you lovely ladies would do me the honor."

Nia stepped over to Jacob and placed her hand on his shoulder turning him so that he would look at her eye to eye. She needed to have his full attention to keep him from seeing her friends laughing at him to his face.

Game For Fame

"Not this time playboy. I need to usher my friends out of the club for a minute. Maybe we can see how you get down later tonight." With that said Laura, Chandelle and Rena threw back their drinks and left the bar arm-in-arm.

"What is going on over there? That woman seems to be losing her mind. She must have hit a big one. Let's go look." Chandelle hurried over to see the commotion with her friends trailing closely behind her. Wow! Nia! Rena! Look! Does that say she just hit for one hundred thousand dollars?" Both women leaned closely to examine what Chandelle was talking about.

"Damn it looks like it." Nia looked amazed. "What I can do with one hundred thousand right through here. It would be the answer to all my prayers."

"You! I can crawl out of this hell hole I'm in. Shit like this always seems to happen to everybody else." Chandelle turned towards Rena fanning herself in disbelief.

"Stop hating Chandelle. It's just not your time yet. You're blessed with your health, a decent job and family and friends who love you."

"I'm not hatin' Rena. I was just saying that I could use that kind of hit right through here that's all." Chandelle stated watching the crowd grow larger as the bells and lights rang louder and brighter.

"We all could use the money. None of us are rich. It was just the tone in which you said it. I'm sorry girl. I don't mean to act like your mother. We all have to figure out how to get out of this rut we're in." Rena searched her purse for a cigarette still watching the woman cry from her new found fortune.

"The country's in a recession." Nia continued. "Everybody's hurting. It's a wonder anybody has any money to gamble at all. But I understand we all have to have some enjoyment. We just gotta be patient and do the best we can. God will see us through this as he has carried us through everything else."

"Oh Boy! Ms. Righteous is on her soapbox. Let us stop and listen to the voice of reason!! Damn Nia can't we wish and wallow in our misery if we want to once in a while? Nobody wants to hear the right thing to do all the time. *There always has to be one in the bunch*. We love you girl but keep that Girl Scout shit to a minimum. We're out trying to have a good time and nobody wants to hear that!" Chandelle heard her name being called. Rachel ran up to the group with a smile plastered across her face.

"Hey guys! I was wondering where you went. I searched the club and couldn't find you anywhere. Mr. Charming went to the bathroom so I decided to walk out to the casino to find you."

"What's going on over there?" Rachel asked.

"Some woman just hit the slot machine for a hundred thousand grand." answered Nia.

"Get the hell outta here! Oh well, some people are born with all the luck. Wouldn't happen to me though cause I'm not sticking my hard earned cash into a slot machine. Hell no!! What are the odds that I'd hit like that? Slim and none and Slim left town long time ago."

"What is with the smile Rachel? Does it have anything to do with Mr. Charming? What's his name and why are you grinning as if you hit the lottery?" Rena asked.

"His name is John. He's single, has a job, never been married, no children and owns his house. So, yes I hit the lottery. He wants to take me to breakfast after the club closes. I wanted to hear what you guys think."

"You're grown Rachel. You know where your comfort level is better than anything we can say to you. Go if you want to. Just be safe and call us in the morning to let us know that you got home safely. Besides, you're saving me gas now that I don't have to drop you off at your house tramp!" Rena hugged Rachel reassuringly.

"Thanks trick. I'll be careful. Well, I'm outta here. My date is probably wondering what happened to me. I'll call you guys tomorrow." Rachel waved goodbye to her friends as they watched her sway happily towards the club.

"Well girls how about we call it a night? I'm tired and I surely don't want to run into that guy that was breathing his dragon breath in my face."

"I am *too* ready to go. There wasn't much to choose from tonight was there? That damn Rachel got the only good lookin' brotha up in there. And as far as you Nia, we're going to send you home to your husband early tonight. Maybe the two of you can still groove to what is left of the evening." Rena dug into her purse to retrieve her keys and headed out to the parking lot.

Chapter 3

Chandelle faintly heard the alarm going off indicating six am and time to get up. Leaning over to silence the alarm, Chandelle hit the snooze button adding fifteen minutes of much needed time to sleep. Five minutes later a loud ringing was heard and Chandelle leaned over to hit the alarm only to realize the ringing didn't stop. *What the…?* Rising from the bed she leaned over to the nightstand to retrieve her phone.

"Hello?"

Will Downing's *Sorry, I* was could be heard playing softly on the other end and she immediately knew who was on the line.

"What do you want Derek? I asked you to lose my number and don't call my house anymore. What part of leave me alone don't you understand? Don't you have some other woman you can harass?"

"Chandy, baby don't treat me like this. It's been four weeks and you haven't returned any of my calls and you won't let a brotha explain what happened. Listen, I'm right outside of your house in the car. Can I see you for a minute? I swear it won't take more than a minute. I promise. Maybe I can give you a ride to work this morning. We really need to talk. C'mon baby… Buzz and let me in." Before Chandelle could protest she heard the other end of the line click. Chandelle walked hesitantly to the door and rang the buzzer allowing the downstairs lock to open. She waited until she could hear Derek begin climbing the stairs before she walked away from the door.

"Chandelle, where are you baby? Come here and let's sit down on the couch for a minute. I know you don't have much time."

Derek sat down on the plush sofa waiting for Chandelle to enter the room. He expected that she was not going to receive what he had to say very well but knew he had to give it a try if he had any hopes of being a part of her life again. After four weeks of the silent treatment, begging and crying wasn't beneath his otherwise cool demeanor. He knew he'd fucked up royally this time but it was time to come clean and hoped it wasn't too late. He knew he shouldn't have lied or kept a secret. Mommy always said it is hard to keep up with a lie because you had to continually tell another one to cover the last. Can't keep track of the lies… Eventually the truth is going to come out. Just better hope you are the one to tell instead of someone else doing it for you or worse. You could get caught with your pants down and then someone is going to get hurt. *Chandelle is the type that will cut your ass. Better tell her Derek.* She warned me over and over and now it's time to face the music.

Chandelle walked into the living room carrying a cup of piping hot Folgers. Sipping she peered over her cup daring him to say a word. Derek knew the look all too well and knew it was better not to say a word but to sit quietly and wait for her to say whatever was on her mind.

"Derek I really don't have time for your shit this morning. I'm due in a meeting in an hour and a half and I haven't even begun to get ready yet. I'm not going to upset myself with rehashing the lie you told me for the last two years we've been together. It's better that you walk out the same way you walked in while you can."

"Chandy baby, I know you're angry but I swear I haven't been lying to you. What we had was real. I'd like to think that you loved me as much as I loved you. We're just so good together that I didn't know how to tell you about my past. I didn't know where to start. I always thought that I had time to tell you and you would understand. It wasn't supposed to come out like it did."

"First of all, my name is Chandelle to you." Placing the cup down on the table, she turned to him giving him her full attention and said, "So what is it Derek? Are you sorry that you didn't tell me or sorry you got caught? You know what? It doesn't even matter anymore. Go call your *wife* and tuck your daughter into bed tonight 'cause I don't have any time

16

or love for you. Listen Derek say whatever it is you have to say because I'm really not feelin' you."

Chandelle headed towards the kitchen for her second cup of coffee. Derek jumped from the couch and grabbed Chandelle by the arm to gain her attention.

"Listen Chandelle, my divorce is final in thirty days. I thought my divorce would be final before you would find out. I was wrong and should have told you before there were a possibility of you finding out from anybody but me. I was going to tell you about my daughter I swear. The divorce was getting ugly. When you and I met I'd already moved out of our house and into the condo downtown. She had the house to raise our daughter in and the only thing that needed settled was visitation and the split of our assets. Now Angela wants to change the terms by demanding a seventy-thirty split and double what was agreed upon in child support. Her demands have moved the decree back thirty days or more."

Pinning her body against the wall and staring into her eyes, he continued,

"I found out all this the morning you came to see me and you saw her leaving my place. She was letting me know that I need to prepare myself for a fight. But it wasn't what you thought. I'm not having an affair with another woman. You were just so happy and you made me believe that I was everything you wanted in a man. For the first time in my life I felt loved and appreciated. I wanted to be that man for you. I wanted to fulfill your dreams and make you happy. I never knew love until you came into my life. How could I risk losing you? It was a bad choice I made but I really believed at the time I was giving us a chance at a life together." Derek leaned his six foot frame down upon Chandelles lips and kissed her deeply.

Chandelle broke the embrace and pushed him away.

17

"No Derek! You kept your secret from me so you lied. How can I ever trust you again?"

Derek pulled Chandelle close to him placing his hand on the small of her back to steady her from running away from him. He began to remove the robe covering her shoulders allowing it to fall to the floor baring a sexy emerald green negligee that caused the already stiff erection between his legs to grow harder aching to be relieved from his pants.

"Derek please! This won't change anything."

"Sshh! Baby, let's enjoy the moment. We can talk later." Derek made a point that Chandelle wasn't eager to argue. Scooping Chandelle into his arms he carried her down the hallway into the bedroom.

Chapter 4

Chandelle walked up Liberty Ave. and Smithfield St. to the cement walkway leading into the revolving doors at McCrory, Brown, and Associates. The company created and sold accounting software and taught firms how to use and engage their software tools for productive accounting practices. Chandelle was one of the firm's top trainers in using the software and periodically assisted in solving problems for software in development. She was hoping that she could get to her office unnoticed by taking the rear escalator to the forth floor being that her office was at the back of the building. Her latest encounter with Derek caused her to miss her Monday morning orientation for prospective clients interested in the accounting software for their human resource departments.

I hope Mr. Brown scheduled one of his corporate board meetings this morning. I can't afford to get caught and written up. Damn! This is the third time this month that I was late for my software class. Hopefully, he'll remember that I was a key player in the quarter of a million dollar software package sold to one of our competitor's major accounts. Well, Derek was worth it. He always had a way of makin' a sista' wanna' smack her mama, cause the shit was that good. A smile crept across her face. *Doggie style in the morning just has a way of getting the juices flowing, slow and steady just the way I like it.* Derek was never a selfish lover and he always aimed to please. *Whew! Let me get my mind right so that I can get a little bit of work done.*

Rrring! Rrring! "McCrory, Brown and Associates Chandelle Carter speaking, can I help you?" *"Chandelle this is Lisa third floor bookkeeping. There seems to be a glitch in the Accounting Pro software program. Can you come down here for a minute?"*

"No problem I'll be right down." Chandelle was called rather frequently when there was a problem with a software program. Her minor in computer programming came in handy and was a plus when it came to job security. Chandelle left her cubicle and made her way down the hallway towards the elevators. Greeting two associates who were also waiting patiently for the elevator to arrive, Chandelle shared good mornings as they entered. The doors opened on the third floor and Chandelle exited and wished the associates a good day. She walked down the hallway to Lisa's office that was located three doors from the conference room where hundreds of thousand dollar sales were negotiated. She continued down the hallway until she approached Lisa's office. Lisa was a cute rather petite blonde with a small frame and the heart of Mother Theresa. Always appreciative of any assistance given to her when she lent a hand, Lisa was also generous when it came to sharing praise. Chandelle was sure she was the cause for her receiving her raise six months ago.

Chandelle knocked and awaited an invitation to enter.

"Come in. How've you been Chandelle?"

"Can't complain. What's going on?"

"This program has my head spinning. I was hoping you might be able to figure out what the hell the problem is."

"Things are changing so quickly in the field I don't see how anybody can really stay abreast of all the changes taking place but I'll give it a shot. What seems to be the problem?"

Chandelle pulled the chair away from the desk and sat down ready to attack whatever it was that was confusing Lisa. She liked Lisa and it was never an issue when it came going downstairs to lend a helping hand.

"Well, if you look at the spreadsheet in front of you, the program requires that all money deposited in a specific time frame would be placed on the left side of the spreadsheet and the liabilities will deduct themselves on the right displaying a line by line description and amount". Lisa used her pencil to illustrate the rows and columns on her twenty-four inch laptop screen.

20

"For some reason all expenditures made by this client in the last six months are tallying but there doesn't seem to be a reflection of money spent in the grand total." Lisa pulled out her calculator and pointed out to Lisa that three hundred thousand dollars was spent in supplies and salaries but the company showed a beginning balance and ending balance of three point two million dollars without making a deposit or withdrawal during the time period in question."

Lisa picked up her phone to call her assistant to make plans for a conference call with their client in the morning. She realized that a potential disaster was in the making and she would need to calm the waters before a major storm hit.

"Ok. So, there is a beginning balance of three point two million dollars. The company spent three hundred thousand dollars but the ledger still says there is a three point two million dollar balance. Hmmph, I'd like to perform this trick for the bank involving my checking account. Chandelle thought to herself.

She knew right away that she was going to need her programming expertise to give her access into the server. The language used to write the Accounting Pro system contained a code that was not only difficult to read but write as well. After gaining entry she slowly realized that fixing the operating system was going to engage hours of networking, resetting of proxy settings and creating a new authentication key. Basically, Chandelle was going to need to rewrite the program in order for it to perform the functions required to keep accurate financial reporting. Interrupting Lisa's phone call, Chandelle asked,

"Lisa, How soon will you need this program repaired before you see the client?

Holding her hand over the mouthpiece of the phone she answered,

"Well I was shooting for Friday so I can meet the clients with their quarterly report by Monday. But if you need the weekend, I can look it over on Monday and be ready to present by Tuesday. Can you have it ready by then?"

Giving the screen a blank stare and thinking she may be in over her head she stated, "Yes, I think so. If not, I can call in a couple of other programmers to help me and do a little overtime. I'll call you and let you know how it's going so you can make your appointment for next week."

Chandelle gathered the program and notes she prepared and left for her office.

She barely made it back to her cubicle when she heard her phone ringing. Usually she transfers her calls to the reception desk so that any emergencies can be forwarded to a colleague or parks all calls so the answering machine can pick them up. Realizing she'd done neither her phone was ringing off the hook.

"McCrory, Brown..." Rena interrupted.

"Hey! What's going on with you? What time are you getting off from work?"

"Hey Rena, what's up girl? I have a project I'm stuck with. I thought I would be able to knock it right out but it is going to be a minute. Why what's going on?"

"Nothing really. Thought you might want to go out for a sip after work that's all."

"I would love to but I can't. But we're going to have to get together. I had a visitor this morning. Need I tell you who was at my door?

"Derek wasn't at your house. You're lying!"

"Yes, he was and I let him in against my better judgment. But I listened to what he had to say and you know what happened." Chandelle heard a scream on the other line.

"Shut up girl! It doesn't mean that we fixed all of our problems. We have a long way to go. I haven't made any promises but I must admit that I *do* miss that man. But he has to prove himself to me and I don't know if I can trust him. We'll see."

"Chandelle do the damn thing! Don't fuck around and lose that man! He loves you and there are too many women out there willing to take him off your hands."

"I hear you. I hear you. I told him that I would call him later so that we can spend some time together and try to work things out. But listen, I gotta go so I can get out of here at a decent hour. I'll call you tomorrow and maybe we can hook up." Chandelle hung up the phone and pushed the red light on her laptop inserting the program disc.

It was two o'clock in the morning and Chandelle was lying across her bed still assessing the program disc given to her eight hours ago.

"This program aint worth shit! I don't know who wrote it and I can't figure out why its not calculating the way it's set up to do. I know my shit and no matter how many times I looked over the configurations everything seems to be in order. But something's not right. I'm sick of this. I need to call Lisa and tell her to inform her client that they hit the jackpot and never have to worry about going broke. They can spend a dollar and don't have to worry about balancing the checkbook. Shit, their board of directors would love them. Frustrated, Chandelle closed her laptop and pushed it to the bottom of her bed. She picked up her remote control and began channel surfing stopping for a commercial advertising the *Rivers Edge*. Chandelle reminisced about being at the casino the previous Friday night and watching a hundred thousand dollar payout being made in front of her. *"Can't stand that Casino. That place robbed me and my girls of enough money that I should be living large right through here. I was so damn stupid thinking I could get a lick to double my money to take care of some things. That place pimped me for more dough than I'd like to think about.*

Game For Fame

Rena and Rachel were coming down highway 376 enjoying *Before I Let Go* by Frankie Beverly and Maze when Rena leaned over to turn down the volume.

"Rachel I gotta tell you something. I'm telling you 'cause I know that out of all my girls you could understand." Concerned Rachel turned facing Rena giving her her full attention.

"What's wrong Rena? Am I going to have to hurt somebody? You know I haven't had to put my thang down in a while. I could use the practice." She said half serious and half joking.

"No *simple* but it is serious. I lost my job today. I don't know what I'm going to do. I was going to cut Ricky loose but I'm going to need him now to pay my rent. From what I heard from a phone conversation of him talking to one of his boys his shit is getting deep. Something about moving product into Ohio and West Virginia. I don't know how big time he is or trying to be but I can't go to jail over his bullshit 'cause he wants to be Scarface." Rachel started laughing.

"I'm serious girl. His cash flow is good and easy but if I was going to do some time it would be 'cause of some crime I committed not something some fool did that I didn't have any parts of. My cousin Jaheim said word on the street is that Ricky was hot. I might have to put his ass out my house. Anyways, I have rent, this car payment, and those credit cards that are sky high. Not to mention I had my mother on my health care plan and she receives a dialysis treatment twice a week. I can get the COBRA plan for six months but that alone is around seven hundred and fifty a month. She has to have her treatments...well... you know the deal" Rena wiped away the tears forming in her eyes.

"Damn Rena. Ok, Back up. How'd you get fired? You never mentioned before you were in jeopardy of losing your job. You had to get warnings or write-ups or something. What happened?" Rena slowed down pulling off the Oakland exit into the Exxon station so she could explain the circumstances.

"It wasn't anything that I did in particular. My position was dissolved. The school district is having financial problems and no longer saw a need for Behavioral Specialists. My job entailed my ability to service the schools and being available to float throughout the entire school district. The superintendent is saying that the counselors based in the schools will make the assessments and if a referral is needed for a more extensive treatment plan they will refer the student to one of the outpatient treatment facilities who offer free services. Ain't that a bitch! My last day is Friday." Rena stated with tears flowing freely.

"Don't cry Rena. We'll figure something out. Push come to shove you can move in with me. You might have to share a room with my niece on the weekends when I have her but you know you have a place to stay." Rachel stated sincerely.

"Thanks, but you know I can't do that. Where would I put my stuff and it's not going to fix my immediate problem in making sure my mother's ok. I can't afford seven hundred and fifty dollars a month."

"Rena. Pay the premium for the COBRA plan. Chandelle, Nia and I will pitch in until you find another job. You have a degree so I'm sure you will find something. At least you have a chance and not stuck in a dead end job like me. I wasn't smart enough to go to college like you and Chandelle. I'll probably be a sales clerk at Macy's 'til I check out of here. Why do you think I am always holding on to every dollar I get? Truth be told why do you think I'm always up on the first brother who looks like he's about something? 'Cause I swear I'm going to find that meal ticket before this body gets old and won't get the attention of a blind man." Rachel took out her compact and began checking her makeup.

"You're a trip!" Smiling Rena continued.

"You make me laugh and you have the nerve to be dead serious with your conceited self. You were able to go to college if you wanted to and you know it. The only reason why you didn't was because your ass is lazy and you wanted to get your party on. Always swore up and down you were going to marry a millionaire. How did you say it? He is going to sweep you away on a white horse and move you into his castle?" she said mocking Rachel.

"Get it right. I said he was going to pick me up in a Rolls and we'd move into his mansion." They both laughed together.

"I feel better Rachel. I love you girl. You always had a way of putting a smile on my face. I'm still scared but I'm just going to have to come up with a plan to keep me afloat until I can find a job. Don't go back and tell anybody what I just said. Chandelle will end up running her mouth and it will get back to my mother. Chandelle's like her other daughter. They're close and I can't afford to have her worried about me as sick as she is."

"I don't agree with keeping my mouth shut but will keep your secret as long as I can. If things get bad though, I can't say I won't tell." Rena nodded started her car and pulled onto Forbes heading towards Shadyside.

Y'vet

Chapter 5

Wednesday morning Judge Charles Cherry left his chamber to preside over the hearing of Washington vs. Washington

"All rise" was heard by the bailiff announcing Judge Cherry's entrance.

"Your honor this is the case of Washington vs. Washington." The bailiff handed the court papers to the judge respectfully.

"Court, you may be seated."

"This shouldn't take long Derek. I read through the papers. The judge will see what Angela is asking for as reasonable. We should be able to reach an agreement before lunch and you can move on with your life." Attorney Jordan Michaels' whispered.

"Your honor my client has issued a fair agreement with an equal division of property and all other marital assets along with a monthly child support payment of eight hundred dollars a month. We feel this is more than adequate to assist Mrs. Washington with the lifestyle she is accustomed to. We also ask for visitation rights on the weekends and equal time during the holidays and summer break." Attorney Michaels' thanked the judge and took his seat.

"Attorney Reed are you ready to proceed?" asked the judge.

"Yes your honor we are. Mrs. Washington asks that she maintain full rights to the family home, half the assets in their respective accounts and supervised visitation by the plaintiff."

"What the hell?!!" Derek yelled from his seat.

"Bang! Bang! Attorney Michaels'! Calm your client or he will be removed from the courtroom!

Ms. Reed is there anything else you would like to add? The judge turned his attention towards the defendants counsel.

"Yes, thank you your honor. Ms Washington is alleging infidelity against the plaintiff and asks that a psychiatric evaluation be completed against Mr. Washington because of prior drug abuse."

Attorney Michaels leaped from his chair to address the court.

"Your honor this is a ploy by the defendant to prolong the proceedings, make a mockery of this court, and tarnishes my clients name and reputation. Mr. Washington used marijuana in his teens long before his marriage and the plaintiff was aware of this. Furthermore, your honor, Mr. Washington was willing to give the home in question to the plaintiff but because of the quick change in the settlement agreement Mr. Washington asks for an equal division of all assets." Judge Cherry glanced down at the agreement.

"Attorney Reed do you have any proof to back up these allegations?"

Picking up a manila envelope from her briefcase she waved them in the air.

"Yes, we do your honor. However, we haven't presented our evidence to the plaintiff and ask for a continuance. Attorney Reed took her seat.

Judge Cherry banged his gavel and stated that the court will reconvene in three weeks.

Attorney Michaels and Derek rose from their chairs and walked towards the back of the courtroom. Derek couldn't believe what had happened.

"Michaels you said that this would be cut and dry. What happened in there? I'm paying you a lot of money to get me out of this marriage and quick. You know she's trying to take me to the cleaners. And this shit about a psychiatric evaluation? That's bullshit man. You have to make this go away. Allegations of drug abuse can ruin my career."

"Calm down Derek and lower your voice. Your outburst can only hurt you not help the situation. Give me time to talk to your wife's attorney to see if we can come to some kind of agreement. In the meantime, wait until you hear from me and stay the hell away from Angela. The last thing we need right now are harassment allegations or worse an order of protection filed against you. Do you understand? Stay the hell away from Angela." Derek pushed past his attorney and out of the courthouse.

Heading towards the parking lot, Derek reached for his keys when he noticed Angela approaching from across the lot.

"Derek no hard feelings, I hope. This is strictly business. What is it they say? If I can't have you nobody will." Angela reached for the door to her car but wasn't quick enough. Derek came up behind her. Leaning into her face he said,

"Angela I don't know what the fuck you're up to but you're fuckin' with the wrong brotha. We made an agreement. You were supposed to take half and leave me the fuck alone." Angela struggled to close the door but Derek held tight.

"I'm warning you Angela. Don't get fucked up and end up with nothing. I'll dig deep, take our daughter, and you ass won't get shit." Derek slammed the door and stood outside her car while she started her engine and pulled into reverse. Angela rolled down her window

"Is that a threat Derek? Does this face look like I give a fuck about your threats? You better back up before you need bail money. Oh, and wait till I give Miss Chandelle a visit. I have a few choice words for her too. Have a good day sweetheart." Angela pulled the car into drive and sped off giving Derek the middle finger.

"Bitch!" Derek walked towards his car eager to get to work to speak to his boss. He hoped to keep a lid on his personal life before it became a problem.

Rachel was leaving the cosmetics counter at Macy's for her lunch break. Passing through the first floor towards the couture section she eyed a red strapless Versace dress on sale. Finding her size she held the dress up and faced the mirror. Behind her she heard a familiar voice.

"Going tricking this weekend?"

"Very funny Chandelle. The dress is sharp ain't it girl? I was thinking about treating myself to it for my date with John this weekend. He wants to take me to the new Jazz club in town." Rachel was studying her reflection in the mirror trying to decide if she was going to use her employee discount and splurge. Rachel loved to shop but she bought clothes that were stylish but could be worn to compliment other pieces. It was rare that she would buy high-end clothes that stood out and she couldn't wear more than once. But she had a gut feeling about John. They hit it off right from the start and shared many of the same interests including the love of jazz.

"Well, you only live once. Get the damn thing. You know you want it." Chandelle reached for the dress to check out the price tag.

"I came down here because I wanted us to get together this weekend. I figured since I was out of the office I would come down here and holla at you. I'm going to call Rena and Nia and ask them to meet at my house Saturday night. Can you make it?" Rachel folded the dress over her arm and headed to the changing room.

"Yeah, I'll be there. Come in while I try this on. I want to tell you something and get your opinion of how this dress looks." Chandelle followed Rachel and sat outside on the bench until she changed into the dress.

"Chandelle, I promised Rena I wouldn't say anything but she and I went out Monday night and she told me that she was fired from her job. She was fucked up behind it. You know she is still dealing with that dude Ricky with his drug- dealing ass. She never got around to putting his ass out of her house. Now that she lost her job you know it's not going to happen anytime soon. I think she's going to stay with him because she needs him to pay her bills. You know you're like a sister to her so I don't have to tell you that her mother needs her treatments if she has hopes of finding a kidney transplant." Rachel opened up the door and walked out of the changing room to see herself in the full length mirror.

"Are you okay Chandelle?" Rachel stared at Chandelle.

"I spoke to her on Monday and she didn't say anything to me about it. I'm wondering why she would keep something like that from me. She knows I would do anything to help her. She doesn't need that asshole. Rena's mom helped raise me so she should know I'll be there for her. I thought we were better than this." Chandelle was searching her purse for her cell phone to call Rena.

"Sshh, Chandelle. Keep your voice down and put your cell phone away. I promised Rena that I wouldn't tell anyone, especially you. She knows you would help her. She's going through some things and she doesn't want to let her mother know. She's afraid that her mother will refuse treatments because her daughter can't afford them. Rena couldn't live with herself if something happened to her mother. Look. The four of us getting together this weekend will be an excuse for us to talk about this without her knowing that I told you. Just keep your mouth shut till then."

"What do you think about the dress?" Rachel turned 360 degrees looking approvingly.

"Okay Rachel." Chandelle said.

"Okay what? The dress looks okay or you won't tell Rena what I told you until we get together this weekend?

"Both. I'll call you before the end of the week. If anything else comes up call me." Chandelle left the dressing room and headed towards the door.

Across town, Nia was picking up her daughters from school.

"Get in girls. Melanie, strap your sister in her car seat and buckle up. I'm running late and I need to drop you girls off at your grandmothers while I go get my hair done." Nia checked her rearview mirrors for oncoming traffic and drove off.

"Mommy! Look over there! Ain't that daddy? Daddy! Daddy!" Slowing for the traffic light Nia looked across the street and saw her husband Tyrik walking towards his car. He turned his attention to the woman beside him and smiled while opening the door so that she could get in.

"Beep the horn Mommy! Daddy doesn't see us!" Shelly yelled eagerly trying to get her fathers' attention.

"Be quiet Shelly! Melanie tightens your sister's seatbelt. Turn around Shelly. That is not your daddy." Nia continued to stare out her window until he drove off. Nia was thinking about changing her plans for the afternoon but decided to drop the girls off and make her hair appointment. *Tyrik better have his shit when he brings his ass home tonight.*

Nia walked into the crowded salon. Fabulous Hair Design's was always crowded. Her standing appointment with Michelle assured her little wait time and guaranteed that she would be in and out in an hour.

33

"Nia. You're right on time. Come back to the bowl so Michael can wash your hair." Nia walked through the waiting room ignoring the dirty looks from the walk-ins hoping to be called back next.

Nia sat down at the bowl, closed her eyes and eased back allowing the water to flow through her hair when she overheard two women talking.

"So Angela, how did it go in court today girl? I know you told that high priced lawyer you want paid from that nigga you married to." Stacy the shampoo assistant asked.

"Derek got his dick cut off today. Should have done it myself when I found out about him and his bitch Chandelle."

Hearing Derek and Chandelle's name grabbed Nia's attention. She began to listen closely to every word. Nia thought about getting up and reaching for her cell phone but decided against it choosing instead to get the whole story.

"My lawyer told them I wanted the house and half of everything. I even brought up his past drug use in high school and asked for a psychiatric evaluation with supervised visits when he visits our daughter."

"Oh Shit! No you didn't girl!! How are you going to bring up some old shit from high school? You're crazy!" Stacy said shaking her head chuckling.

"Motherfucker thinks he can walk out on me and live comfortably while I have to take care of his child and find a job? I don't think so. Sick of these men thinking they can do whatever they want whenever they want. He comes home and tells me that he doesn't love me no more and we grew apart. Yeah, I guess we did grow apart. I'm at home playing mommy and not working while he's in college. As soon as he betters himself I'm not good enough. Fuck that! I'm going to get mines!" Angela closes her eyes and waits for her final rinse.

"I heard that! Did you have to use your secret weapon? Stacy pulled the lever on the stool allowing Angela to raise her head from the bowl.

"My lawyer flashed the envelope in court but the papers and photos weren't given to the judge. She said that Derek and his lawyer have the right to view the material first before going before the judge. He needs to allow me to have the house and the money. Once those photos are released the judge won't give him shit. Angela said with a smirk on her face.

"Well, just know what your doing is all I have to say. Better not go to that mans' job. We been friends for years Angela and you know I want the best for you. Just don't fuck up what you got. How will you expect to get those monthly checks if the man isn't working?" Stacy wrapped the towel around Angela's head to escort her to the stylist.

"Oh, I'm not going to fuck up. Besides, who said anything about going to his job? You know what I mean?" Angela got up and winked at Stacy as they walked towards the stylist chair for her blow dry and curl.

Damn! This is the day from hell! My husband was supposed to be in a meeting all day in Cranberry, forty-five minutes from here and I see him leaving the Hill District at one o'clock in the afternoon with some trick. Now I overhear some bitch planning to do harm to one of my girls? Oh, Hell No! None of this shit is going to go down like this.

"Nia? Are you ready? The chair's open for you." the assistant informed her. "Please come this way." Nia followed contemplating her next move.

Game For Fame

Chapter 6

Close to quitting time Chandelle was at her desk reviewing the Accounting Pro program given to her the previous weekend by Lisa. After checking the program for errors, she figured it easier to rewrite the program to function properly so that it could be ready for the presentation on Tuesday. Chandelle still couldn't figure out why it didn't function as it was previously written. She decided to copy the program and work on it in her spare time as one of projects. It was an opportunity to sharpen her programming skills and have an ace in the hole if needed when she needed an excuse to explain why she was late.

Mr. Brown I know I'm late and I'm sorry but I was up all night working on this program. I wanted to correct this before it cost the company any embarrassment or worse thousands of dollars. Please come into my office and allow me to demonstrate what I'm talking about... Yeah, that'll do it. Chandelle smiled to herself and tucked the program away neatly into her briefcase.

"Excuse me Chandelle. Can I speak with you for a minute? Chandelle looked up from her desk to see Mr. Brown the owner of the company standing in her cubicle.

"Yes, Mr. Brown please come in and sit down. Can I get you something? Coffee maybe?" Chandelle quickly rose from her chair and offered him a seat.

"No. I just want to remind you that starting time is eight o'clock and I expect you to be at your desk at that time. You arrived close to nine am on Friday and you were an hour late Monday morning. I meant to speak with you then when I found out you didn't teach your class, but I got held up in a meeting. Need I remind you that you can't afford another write up this quarter? I understand that you did a fantastic job helping bookkeeping with an accounting program and it's very much appreciated. You have proved to be a team player and a valued employee but your tardiness can be grounds where I would have to let you go. This is your last warning Ms. Carter." Mr. Brown folded his hands across his lap and crossed his legs awaiting an explanation.

"I understand Mr. Brown. It won't happen again." Chandelle subtly held her breath then breathed a sigh of relief when he abruptly got up and left.

Shit, I better get my act together. I can't afford to lose my job. My best friend needs me and I have a wedding that I hope to be planning in the next year. Derek has a good paying job but a sister needs her own money and he can't afford to take care of me on his salary. Let me get my ass outta here. I need a drink.

Chandelle pulled into the *River's Edge* parking lot and quickly found a space on the third level. It was sheer luck to park and have the ability to walk the ramp directly into the casino. Wednesday nights were a good night but because the casino offered free drinks but between five and nine pm it was sometimes crowded. Chandelle knew it was a ploy to lure in the customers because very few people were able to go out on a Wednesday night and expect to make it in to work the next day. Chandelle walked in looked around and decided to drink at the bar. Two drinks were her limit and if she planned on gambling she could do so at the bar. Chandelle signaled the waiter.

"Rum and Coke please." Looking through her wallet she placed a dollar bill on the bar for the tip.

"Excuse me Miss, would you like to have this seat? I'm leaving." The gentleman seated next to her stated.

"Yes, thank you." Chandelle took off her jacket and placed it around the back of the stool making herself comfortable.

"I left this machine warmed up for you. It should be ready to give you a jackpot." The older gentlemen smiled swallowed the remainder of his drink and walked away.

The waiter set down a napkin and placed her drink down in front of her.

"Will that be all mam?"

"Yes. Thank you. I'll call you when I'm ready for round two" Chandelle looked down at the machine in front of her. Five games where available to choose from. Five card draw poker was one of her favorites. She remembered learning how to play poker as a little girl from watching her father and his friends on Saturday nights. Slipping a twenty in the machine, Chandelle waited for her credits to wrack up. She bet four credits equaling a dollar on her first hand. King of spades, Jack of Diamonds, Ten of spades, King of Diamonds and a Deuce of Clubs were dealt out. Chandelle decided to keep the pair and draw for three cards. King of Clubs, Nine of hearts and a Three of spades gave her three of a kind. Ding! Ding! Ding! *Oh! I Hit!! Twenty-five dollars! I needed that!* Chandelle sat staring at the screen as her point s racked up. *Damn! I forgot to insert my Players Club card. I need all the casino credits I can get.* Digging in her purse Chandelle located the card and placed it into the slot. Pressing her five- digit password on the keypad the monitor read: **Welcome to the Rivers Edge Chandelle Johnson. You have three hundred and sixty-five credits towards free play.** *Yes! This machine did give me the credits for my hit! Let me go cash out my twenty-five dollars and play with the free credits. Maybe tonight is my lucky night!* Chandelle folded her coat over her chair and asked the bartender to watch her seat until she returns. Making her way to the cashier she cashed out her winnings and received a code so that she can retrieve her bonus play from the machine.

Two hours have passed and Chandelle lost her bonus credits, spent her twenty-five dollars in winnings and added fifty more dollars to her loss. *How can I be so damn stupid and get caught up like this? I should no better than to think I can chase my money and break even. The house is supposed to win. I can never walk away a winner. I'm taking this card out of this machine. These people are probably tracking how much money I spent and no that I will spend every dime I have 'cause I always do this dumb shit! As much money as I have spent in this joint I should be playing on them. Too bad I don't have more credits on this card so I can have a chance to win my money back. Where's Accounting Pro now when you need it…Oh Shit!!!*

Nia was putting away the leftovers from dinner when she heard Tyrik come into the house. Hearing the clanging of dishes being placed in the dishwasher, Tyrik walked to the kitchen and placed his briefcase on the kitchenette stool.

"Hey baby. I'm hungry whatcha cook for dinner tonight? He walked towards his wife kissing her on the cheek.

"Whatever McDonalds is serving." Nia closed the dishwasher door and pressed the wash cycle.

"What do you mean whatever McDonald's is serving? You didn't have to work today. Your husband can't get a home cooked meal? What's wrong Nia? You act like you have an attitude." Tyrik walked towards the refrigerator and grabbed a beer. Popping the lid he took a sip before speaking,

"Now maybe you can understand why I don't come home early anymore. It's easier for me to stay late at the office and stop somewhere and grab a sandwich. And you wonder why we ain't spending any quality time together. Our marriage is falling apart because of you. You used to know how to treat your man." Nia slammed the dishwasher door closed and turned to face her husband.

"You're a damn lie! The only thing you're working on is that bitch I saw you with earlier! I saw you this afternoon on Centre Avenue. You were with your bitch and you looked real comfortable to me. You said that you had a sales meeting in Cranberry today. How the fuck you end up on the Hill? I asked a week ago if there was someone else and you said no. If you want to be with someone else then go but don't try to make a fool out of me. I'm not going to stay with a man just for the sake of having one. Can't make someone want you who doesn't want to." Nia swung landing a smack to his jaw.

'What the fuck is wrong with you?" Tyrik grabbed Nia's hands and backed her against the wall pinning her hands above her head.

"I'm not going to tell you this again. If you act like a dude Imma treat you like a dude." He threw her hands to her side and walked to the bedroom. Nia followed closely behind screaming and cussing.

"So, what? You're not even going to try to deny it Tyrik? Who is she? Don't run now! Your ass got busted and now you want to run. I'm sitting around this house thinking that I'm not putting enough time into our marriage and believing this is my fault. Here I am trying to scrounge up new business and taking care of the kids. Thinking that maybe not paying enough attention to your no good ass and here you are running around the streets with a bitch that looks like she just graduated from high school. Our girls were in the backseat of the car yelling, Daddy! Daddy! And I'm covering for your cheating ass saying it wasn't you. They're getting older Tyrik. They ain't stupid. Is this the example you want to give our kids?" Tyrik pushed passed Nia to the closet to get his clothes and overnight bag. Hearing that his girls had witnessed his infidelity he was overcome by guilt and remorse. *Damn! I swear I didn't want this to come out. He thought to himself.*

"Nia I'm out. I'll let you know where I'm at in case you need me. I need to get away. I just need some to think and clear my head. I'll call the girls tomorrow." Tyrik grabbed his clothes and headed out the door.

"I don't know if there will be a place for you to come back to Tyrik." Nia said slamming the bed room door closed. Tyrik thought about turning around and begging for forgiveness but decided against it until he thought about how to handle the mess he was in.

41

Game For Fame

Derek laid across his king size bed flipping through the stations searching for anything that would take his mind away. His soon to be ex-wife had become a problem he knew that a simple divorce wasn't going to handle. Threatening that if she can't have him nobody will was something to take serious when it came to Angela. It wasn't the first time she would have made good on a threat. A year ago she put rat poison in the neighbor's dog bowl because she thought the attractive young woman living next door was trying to get in Derek's pants. Poor woman came home from work to find the dog dead with his legs straight up in the air with a note attached to his collar saying *Don't let the police find your ass dead with your pants down and legs wide open.* The police were called to her house and she moved out a couple of weeks later. Derek asked Angela about it after the rumors about what happened to the dog spread through the neighborhood. She swore she had nothing to do with it. *I know that bitch was the one who did that to that dog. I didn't speak to her for two days before that shit happened cause she swore I was doing something with the woman. I should've left her then. Now she is threatening to do some dumb shit. I don't know what she is up to but this shit gotta stop. I have to figure out a way to get my daughter away from her crazy ass. If I don't figure out a way to fix this Chandelle will never come back to me.* Derek placed the remote on the end table and picked up the phone to call Chandelle. Trying her home phone the answering machine picked up. Deciding not to leave a message he dialed her cell phone in hopes of reaching her.

"Hey baby, how are you?" Derek smiled into the phone grateful that she answered his call after weeks of the silence treatment. He knew going to her house Monday morning was the only chance of putting their relationship back together.

"I'm fine Derek. I was going to call you when I got home. I just left the casino. I stopped to have a drink. Hold on while I pull over at the convenience store. I need to pick up a loaf of bread and we can talk." Pulling into the seven-eleven, Chandelle put the car in park and placed the phone to her ear.

"Okay. So what happened in court today? Is it over?"

"No baby. It's going to take a little longer than I planned. She made some allegations in court today about drug use. Before you say anything, you know Angela and me was together in high school and then got married a couple of years later. I smoked a little weed back then and she brought that shit up in court to prolong the divorce. Now I may have to have a psychiatric evaluation in order to see my daughter. She doesn't want to let it go and thinks that I will give in and go back to her." Derek got up from his bed and begun pacing the floor.

"A psychiatric evaluation? Is she trying to say you're and addict or crazy or something? Look Derek. I love you but I am not dealing with any drama between you and your ex wife. If you would've been honest with me from the start maybe things wouldn't be as bad as they are now and I could've been a little more supportive. But as things are right now, I can't deal. When you have your divorce situation all straightened out you can holla at me then. I need to get myself together right now anyway. My boss is on my ass at work and my best friend needs me right now. So let's just give this time to heal and then we can talk. Chandelle pulled her keys from the ignition and placed them in her purse.

"Chandelle, I know this is a fucked up situation but we don't have to break up over this. I thought this morning proved to you how much I love you and want to be with you. You know that there's no love between Angela and me. Don't let her come between us he stated pleading.

"Derek, I'm not saying that we won't be together. I'm just asking you to handle your business with her first. I have too much shit going on right now to add your drama to the mix. When you settle things with her then we can talk okay? I'll talk to you tomorrow." Chandelle got out the car to get her bread and head home. She had other things on her mind like the Accounting Pro program and testing to see if her theory was correct.

Across town Ricky was meeting with his boy Tre at the holdup house where they were counting money and discussing the plan to divide two kilos and expanding their territory. Ever since Raymond was busted with twenty bricks of cocaine and two million dollars his territory was left wide open for anybody to come in and take over. Ricky's new supplier fronted him a brick and let him buy one at half the price allowing Ricky to move from his number two position to the boss on the West side all the hustlers in the street reported to.

"Ricky man, we need a new spot for us to set up. I'm not trying to question your authority cause you're the reason we came up. But I don't think that it is a good idea to stash at your girls place. She ain't down with the game and she may fuck up and have the wrong niggas in her crib and we end up losing everything. Word got back that one of her peoples is asking too any questions about you man. Plus we have too many soldiers on the streets that know about this spot so we can't have this kind of weight laying around here either. I was thinking, I got that place over on nineteenth nobody knows about and I can stash these bricks there till we put a plan in place." Tre said placing twenties in the bill counter to be counted and sealed.

Tre and Ricky have been boys since they were teens on the corners of the North Side. Tre took a bullet for Ricky one day when two corner hustlers from the East Side tried to rob them. Tre was able to shoot the driver before he made off in his car. Tre pushed Ricky out the way before taking one in his right leg allowing Ricky to keep their stash and get away. By the time the police arrived Ricky was home safely with the days take while Tre was taken to the hospital claiming a drive by shooting was the reason for the assault. The two had been tight ever since. Ricky and Tre have been inseparable slinging and making moves. Problem was Tre was getting cocky and taking niggas out if he thought they were talking too much or taking money off the top. Tre was wrong sometimes but didn't give a fuck and believed that niggas would think twice before running their mouths or stealing from them. *You gotta make examples out of some of these niggas Ricky so they respect you* he'd later say. It was becoming difficult to find young hustlers willing to put in some work for them in fear of Tre's reputation. Word on the street was that if the money was coming up short it was Tre taking the profit so he could start an empire of his own. Tre knew he would have to bring in his own people because he didn't have the street respect or know the supplier. So naturally, Ricky with his cooler demeanor and street smarts was next in line after Raymond was locked up to call all the shots and become the next hood legend.

"I got this man. My woman knows what's up. She knows I'm out on these streets hustling to keep our money tight. She doesn't know how much is in the crib or where I put it but she knows I'm dirty and she ain't stupid to cut off her ends. Once we get this delivery cooked and divided it amongst the playas, I should have a spot set up." Ricky placed the bundles of cash in a duffle bag and zipped it up throwing it over his shoulder.

"I'm out. Handle the rest of this money man. I gotta make a run so I'll hit you up later." Ricky showed his boy love with a pound and headed out the door.

*Yeah I'm gonna handle some of this money son. You slippin man. Takin things too lightly cause Raymond is down. The streets are getting sloppy and I got a plan to tighten this shit up. I'm your boy but...*Tre bagged up the remainder of the money placing it in the other duffle bag for delivery and placing twenty thousand in a backpack for himself.

Chapter 7

It had been a month since Rachel had a date and she was nervous about going out later that evening. John called three times confirming their date and asked that she dress to the nines because he made special plans. It hadn't been since she was in her twenties that she could remember a man sweatin' her. *Maybe John is the one. We have a lot in common and from talking to him all night every night this week, he seems to want a serious relationship as much as I do. I swear if this doesn't work out I'm seriously going to think about taking some night courses at the community college. After hearing what happened to Rena I am going to need a back up plan. The only way that is going to happen is if I have a plan B.* The doorbell rang interrupting her thoughts. Rachel stepped out of her bedroom and down the hallway to answer her door. Looking out the peephole, John stood with a bottle and flowers in his hand. *Hmm, on time and bearing gifts. He definitely gets a brownie point.* Rachel unlocked the door and greeted John with a kiss on his cheek.

"Hi. How are you? Come in." Rachel stepped away from the door allowing John entry into the living room.

"Hey baby. You look beautiful." John extended his hand giving Rachel the flowers and bottle of wine.

"I brought this for you. I was hoping that you can chill the wine and maybe we can share a night cap after we leave the club."

"Thanks. I'll take this and put it in the refrigerator for later. Can I get you something before we head out? She stated while walking towards the kitchen.

"No. I was hoping we could leave a little early and maybe stop and get something to eat." John made himself comfortable picking up the pictures on the fireplace mantle. One particular picture caught his eye. Rachel was seated on a bench at what looked like a bar-b-que. Behind her was an attractive gentleman with his arm around her shoulders and kissing her on her cheek. Rachel walked into the living room noticing John eyeing the pictures.

"Hey, you ready to go?" She stated startling his concentration on the photo in his hand.

"That is a picture of me and my ex boyfriend. That was a special time. We were at the park celebrating my parents' fiftieth wedding anniversary." Rachel walked towards John smiling and reminiscing about the moment the photo was taken.

"I would think that if he's your ex you would have gotten rid of this picture by now. How are you gonna have a brotha take you seriously if u have this nigga' sittin' up on your mantle like your still kicking it?" John handed the photo to Rachel and turned to walk away towards the door.

"Are you ready Rachel? Get your coat and I'll meet you out at the car." John stepped out the front door allowing it to slam behind him.

Dumbfounded, Rachel stared at the door. *What the fuck is up with that? I know he's not trippin about some old boyfriend five years ago... Okay girl. Get it together. It's just not that serious.*

Arriving at the Jazz club, John was once again the perfect gentleman. His demeanor was pleasant sparking conversations between set performances and serving up compliments along side the drinks. It was as though his demeanor changed completely forgetting about the incident in the apartment just a few hours before. He was generous insuring that her glass was never empty and had a song dedicated to her before the night ended because the pianist was a friend he grew up with from the old neighborhood.

47

Game For Fame

"Rachel you ready to head out of here? I thought maybe we can go back to your place and enjoy that bottle of wine I brought earlier? John got up and walked towards Rachel to help her out of her chair.

"Yes. I'm ready. That wine sounds good right through here. Let's go." Rachel puts on her coat and they head towards the door. The short drive home lasted only ten minutes before they turned into her complex.

"Come in and make yourself comfortable." Opening her door Rachel took his coat and reached for the remote control from the coffee table and turned on the CD player selecting some smooth jazz to continue the mood from the club.

"I'll go in and get some glasses and the wine. Have a seat on the couch." Yelling from the kitchen Rachel said,

"I had a really nice time John. Can I get you something to eat with the wine?" When he didn't answer, Rachel walked towards the living room to find John naked laying across her couch stroking what had to be at least ten inches of pleasure to attention.

"John! What the hell...?" Rachel stood in shock not able to look away but not wanting him to stop stroking what looked so good and had her panties wet with eagerness. It's been over a month since Rachel had been sexed real good and she was tired of playing partner to a plastic dick that didn't talk back.

"I thought that we'd skip the wine and get down to business. I was checking out how you been eyeing me all night. I know you want this. Come here and ride daddy." Hesitantly Rachel walked closer to get a better look. She knew the risk in sleeping with John. She really liked him and believed that if you sleep with a man on the first date, chances were that you'd never hear from him again. *Damn! Fine and packing? I gotta go for this. I'm just going to have to take the risk. I'm about to cum just watching him play with himself.* Slowly Rachel began to unzip the back of her dress allowing it to fall to the floor. Giving John a show she turned around showing him her big round ass, then bent over slowly pulling down her thigh high fishnets as she grabbed her ankles. John turned her around pulling down her thong and placing his fingers between her thighs finding the moisture of her vagina fingering her to gain easy access for entry. Reaching for his pants, John pulled a condom from his pocket.

"Slide the condom on baby and get on top." Ripping open the packet, Rachel slid the condom down his shaft and climbed on top bucking and sweating until she was about to reach her first climax. Climbing off his dick, Rachel crawled onto the floor raising her ass high in the air.

"Hit it from behind baby. Fuck me hard! Make me cum! John jumped from the couch eager to hit it doggy style. Mounting her he thrusted, grunting with each stroke.

"Talk to me baby. Is it good? Talk to me!! Oh Shit! I'm cumming baby! Oh Keisha!! Yes!" John fell backwards exhausted trying to catch his breath.

"Who the fuck you just call me mother fucker? Rachel jumped up from the floor and stood over John as he gained his composure.

"Huh?" John slid on his ass backing away from Rachel. Stepping on his pants so he couldn't reach to get dressed, she picked up the glass vase containing the flowers he bought earlier. Rachel poured the vase of water on John causing him to jump from the chill. She then threw the vase narrowly missing his head.

"Who the fuck is Keisha? How the fuck you gonna lay up with me and call me some other bitch's name? Get the fuck out my house! Now mother fucker!" Rachel ran to the couch and retrieved his shirt then his pants and shoes from the floor. She walked to the door throwing his clothes into the parking lot.

"Get the fuck out now before I call the police." Walking towards the door John said,

"Your gonna get upset cause I slipped and called you my ex girlfriends name but you have your exes picture up on the mantle front and center. You need to clean house before you get an attitude baby. But let me say this, you need to bottle and sell that shit between your legs." Rachel slammed the door and ran to the bathroom crying.

Chapter 8

Chandelle was frying up the last of the wings when she heard her doorbell ring. Checking the time she realized that is was seven o'clock and she was late getting herself together in time for her girls to arrive. She walked to the door and opened it to see Rena and Rachel standing in the doorway with a case of beer and what looked like chips and pretzels in a shopping bag.

"Come in ladies. You didn't have to bring any snacks. I fried chicken all afternoon and I don't want any leftovers when you leave. Come in the kitchen and help me carry this food to the dining room table."

"What's going on Chandelle? Chicken smells good and I'm hungry. Rachel asked while placing a few beers in the refrigerator.

"I made some potato salad and greens too. Help me put this food out." Rachel grabbed the chicken while Rena followed with the potato salad and greens and Chandelle carried the plates and utensils. Rachel grabbed a chicken wing off the plate and took a seat at the table.

"Damn Rachel you weren't lying when you said you were hungry. Slow down. That food ain't goin anywhere." Rena said staring at Rachel chow down on her wing.

'Whatever. I said I was hungry. That's why I stopped at the store for snacks in case Chandelle didn't have any food up in here. Anyway, Chandelle how are you and where's Nia's ass? I haven't talked to that girl all week" Chandelle took a seat across from Rachel and began fixing a plate.

"I spoke with her briefly earlier today. She said she'd be here after she dropped the kids off at her mothers. " As Chandelle bit into her chicken, the doorbell rang.

"Rena, can you get that please? It's nobody but Nia." Rena walked down the hallway to answer the door.

"Hey Nia. How are you?

"I'm okay. Got some shit going on but I'll tell you about it in a minute. Where's Chandelle?

"She's in the dining room." Rena hurriedly followed behind Nia to get the scoop.

"Hey, Nia. What's up girl? We were just talking about you. Nobody heard from you all week. Chandelle noticed with concern that something was going on with her girl.

"What's going on?" Chandelle asked.

"Everything is going on. Tyrik left earlier this week." Nia began fumbling around in her purse for a cigarette and lighter.

"What do you mean he left earlier this week? Left as in business trip or left you?" Rachel asked.

"He left me. I didn't even have the chance to put his ass out. I saw him with this young girl earlier that day when he told me that he had a meeting to go to for work. The kids were in the car yelling for his ass. I told them that it wasn't him. But you know they knew better." Nia stated as tears rolled down her face.

"What? You didn't tell us that Tyrik was fooling around. I mean when we went out last weekend you said the two of you were having some issues but I didn't think it was this bad. I was just thinking it was the normal everyday bullshit couples go through. I was running my mouth about Ricky and here you were dealing with some deep shit by yourself." Rena said rubbing Nia on the back.

"I wasn't sure then. He has been acting distant and not coming home at the usual time. I asked him if there was someone else and he said no. He told me that I was too busy for my husband and wasn't giving him the attention that he needed. Here I thought it was something I wasn't doing and his trifling ass was out hoeing."

"You knew his ass was going to deny it. They always do. Need I remind you about Derek?" Chandelle stated.

"She doesn't need to hear that shit Chandelle. We're talking about a marriage here and two little girls. She had to believe her husband or at least give him the benefit of the doubt." Rena said offering Nia a box of tissues.

"Of course you would say that Rena. Your ass is knee deep with some nigga you can't get rid of cause you're always trying to justify some bull shit." Chandelle said giving Rena the eye letting her know she knew what was up with her situation.

"Oh hold up baby. First of all, we're supposed to be supporting Nia and second of all this isn't about me. I know you ain't trying to put my shit out there like I'm hiding from what's going on with Ricky. I knew he dealt drugs and I'm aware that I was with him for the money. Ain't no shame in my game. I'm just trying to find an easy way to get out so nobody gets hurt. You need to check yourself. At least I'd know if I was running around with a married man. After two years you can't tell me you didn't know anything. Now who is fooling who?" Immediately, Rena began to feel bad and wished she could've taken back her last comment but Chandelle needed to come off her high horse.

"Stop it before the two of you stop speaking for a month like the last time over something stupid." Rachel said turning her attention back to Nia.

"So Nia go ahead."

"I confronted him about being with that girl and he didn't deny it. So, I slapped the shit out of him and that's when he went to the bedroom and started packing his clothes. The only time his dogg ass felt some guilt was when I brought up the girls and them witnessing his trifling ass with that woman. He said that he needed to leave and think about things and what he wanted to do and would speak to the girls later. He then up and walked out. Can you believe that shit? The motherfucker acts like he has the option to decide whether he wants to stay in this marriage or not. He should have thought about that shit before he lay down with that tramp." Nia stated blotting her eyes and growing angry.

"I know you're mad and hurt Nia but you really need to think about this before you go off making some decisions you may later regret. You have to consider those kids and right now you aren't in a position to carry that household by yourself. You can't afford it. Not to mention that you are still in love with the man. Now ain't that right?" Rachel said looking for backup from Rena and Chandelle. Chandelle turned her head and stared at the floor as if she didn't hear a word Rachel just said. Rena looked at Nia and stated,

"I agree with Rachel. It's still too early to make decisions right now. The two of you just need to take this time apart from one another and decide if your marriage is worth saving. It is so easy to throw what's important away thinking that we can start over or another great thing is going to come along not realizing the damage and hurt we cause from making hasty decisions. Give it some time Nia. We are all here to support you in any way we can." Rena put her arms around Nia and gave her a big hug.

"Thanks. I appreciate what you are trying to do but I still can't see trying to make this work. If he wasn't going to deny it and only made a move because he got caught, I don't know if I can trust him. I'd appreciate how he felt if he would've left first and then had his little fling. At least he would've been honest." Nia said lighting another cigarette.

54

"I doubt that's true Nia. You still would've been hurt and if he had the affair after he left you, you would then claim he was planning to be with her all along or that he was with her before he left you and was just waiting for the right moment to leave. Your feelings would hurt the same. So give it some time before you make a decision you might regret later." Rena rose from the table to head towards the kitchen.

"Anybody want a beer? I need a drink plus there is something I want to tell you." Rena left for the kitchen returning with a six pack in her hand.

"I want you all to know that I lost my job. I had a chance to tell Rachel and I saw this as good as time as any to tell the two of you." Rena looked over at Chandelle and her suspicions of Chandelle knowing her situation were correct by look on her face.

"What took you so long to let me know? If anybody should know it should be me. We grew up as sisters and I know the responsibilities you are carrying with paying your bills and taking care of you mom. So what's the plan Rena? Or need I ask? I hope you're not banking on that asshole to take care of you."

"Well, not forever. I am giving my self some time to find another job but I don't have any choice right now. The insurance premium I have to pay to make sure mom gets her treatments cost more than my rent and car insurance payment alone. So, it is what it is. I just wanted you to know." Rena took a sip of her beer and began moving her fork around her plate waiting for Chandelle to show her ass.

"What do you mean what choice do you have?! You need to put his ass out! You heard about what is going on in the street and Ricky is about to make some moves you don't need to be involved with. If he gets busted homelessness will be the least of your problems. Put his ass out now while you can. I have some money saved and can help you for a little while until you find a job." Chandelle said.

"I'll think about it Chandelle. You can't afford to take care of me I won't feel right taking your money. Plus, shouldn't you be trying to save for your wedding? Rena stated sincerely.

"I'd rather give it to you now for bills then try to spend it trying to bail your dumb ass out of jail. As far as wedding, there isn't going to be one if Derek doesn't get his shit together with that soon to be ex wife of his."

"Speaking of ex wife, Chandelle I have something to tell you about Derek's ex." Chandelle glanced at Nia with a perplexed look on her face. She wasn't sure that Nia even knew who Derek's wife was.

"The other day I went to the hairdresser and I overheard your name while I was getting my hair washed. This chick was getting her hair washed in the next bowl and was talking to the shampoo girl about her and her husband. The shampoo girl asked how their day in court went and she said that her lawyer put her thing down against the plaintiff and his name was Derek Washington. Well, you knew immediately that caught my attention. Anyway, she continued talking about how she was going to bleed him for every cent he had and keep him from seeing their daughter. Then the bitch was asked how she was going to make him give her what she wanted and she alluded to going through the woman he was seeing. Chandelle, that's when she mentioned your name. I was going to call you then but changed my mind so that I can concentrate on her and make sure I didn't miss a word she said. So, I decided to call you when I got home but you know what happened after that. I'm sorry I didn't tell you earlier." Chandelle arose from her chair and began clearing the table.

"Are there any more secrets we need to get out in the open? Sorry, I don't mean to be smart. Don't worry about it Nia. I understand. That bitch better know what she's dealing with. I don't have time for her childish games. As far as I'm concerned everything is out in the open. He swore they were separated when we got together so he just needs to settle things between them if he wants to have a future with me. End of story." Chandelle and her friends grabbed their beers to relax in the living room.

Chapter 9

Chandelle had a huge fifty-two inch television set, a surround sound music system and two large sofas for entertaining her guests.

"Did Derek fight you against breaking up the relationship? I know he wasn't trying to let you go without a fight Chandelle" Rachel said while flipping through the CD collection and choosing to play SADE softly in the background.

"Yeah, he had a problem with it. But like I told him, we aren't through. I still plan to be with him but he needs to get his shit in order first. I don't even know that woman he's married with and her ass is in the beauty shop talking shit on me. I don't have that to do. He needs to handle it. But…" Before Chandelle could finish her thought the doorbell rang. She reached to answer and looked out the peephole but no one was there. A manilla envelope was slid under the door and Chandelle reached down to pick it up and checks its contents.

"What's that Chandelle? Rachel said peering over Chandelles shoulder.

"I don't know. I looked outside but I didn't see anyone at the door or who left it." Chandelle noticed her name printed on the outside with her full name and address. She ripped open the envelope and took out the letter that read:

Stay the fuck away from my husband bitch! I'm only going to tell you once. I don't know what Derek did or didn't tell you which is why I am being nice enough to give you a warning. I sent the enclosed pictures to your job so your boss has an idea what type of lady he has representing him to his clients. I'm sure you won't have a job after your

boss gets these but consider yourself lucky I didn't do something worse. Talk to Derek and I'm sure he will tell you what I'm capable of.

With all my love, Angela

Chandelle dropped the letter to the floor and searched the envelope for the pictures inside. Rena picked up the letter to find out what had Chandelle in a state of shock. One by one Chandelle flipped through the pictures. Derek was lying across a bear skin rug in front of a fireplace nude in various sexual positions. What took her by greater surprise was that the woman fucking her man wasn't her but a white woman with long blonde hair and a tattoo on her shoulder of a heart with an arrow going through the middle. Chandelle recognized the woman from the company Christmas party held at the Hilton hotel the past year. Her name was Brenda Morrelli. She was the wife of Derek's boss. The following three pictures were of him and the woman she recognized leaving Derek's condo the day she paid him a surprise visit. She assumed she was Angela, the bitch who wanted a serious ass kicking. The following pictures bothered her more than the previous. They were pictures of her and Derek having sex in his apartment. *What the fuck am I dealing with? I know Derek wouldn't hide a camera and secretly take pictures of us.*

"Chandelle! What the fuck is going on! This bitch is crazy! She said she was being nice then turns around and threatens you with some pictures to your boss? She needs to be dealt with. Let me see those pictures." Rena passed the letter to her friends and reached for the pictures from Chandelles hand. Chandelle stood in a daze staring at the wall in front of her in what seemed to be deep thought.

"Damn Chandelle! Do you know these people? How the fuck did she get pictures of you and Derek having sex? He's not in on this with her cause you called things off with him? Chandelle?! Snap the fuck out of it and get a grip! Did you hear what I said?" Rena grabbed Chandelle by the arm and led her to the couch. *Chandelle is acting too cool. She was just*

going off on me about Ricky and upset about Nia's situation. She's shook but…
Rena thought to herself

"Get my phone. I need to call Derek's ass right now". Rachel grabbed the phone from the mantel and handed it to Chandelle. Chandelle dialed Derek's home and cell phone numbers but when he didn't answer she left him a message telling him to call her no matter what time he got in.

"So, what do we do next Chandelle? I'm ready to go give that bitch a visit. Obviously she's crazy. Read the note again. She says she's being *nice* but then says she sent the pictures to your job. I'm telling you she's crazy. Some *Fatal Attraction* shit." Rena asked ready to make a move out the door.

"Sit down Rena. She is crazy. Derek told me about some dumb shit she done in the past. That was part of the reason why I told him to handle his business with her before we went any further. He said she done some questionable shit but he was never able to prove it. I just need to get in touch with him and get some answers before I make my next move. If she sent those pictures to my boss, I may not want to go into work on Monday. Today is already Saturday and I need to buy myself some time. Mr. Brown can't fire me until he sees me so if I use some vacation time I can come up with a plan B. I need a steady income right through here and that bitch needs dealt with. I just need to know if her threats are real." *Yeah that bitch needing dealt with is what worries me.* Rena thought keeping a close eye on Chandelles demeanor.

"This is some fucked up shit. Everything is fucked up. I feel hopeless right now and you know that's not like me at all. I always have faith that things are going to be okay but right now I just don't know. The three of us are going through some shit and none of us are in the position to help the other. Rachel, count your blessings that you ain't dealing with any drama." Nia said.

"Well with everything that is going on, I didn't want to tell you what happened last night. My shit is lightweight compared to what you're dealing with." Chandelle, Nia, and Rena looked at Rachel as if she couldn't be serious.

"You know I had that date with John last night. We went out and had a relatively good time until we got back to my house. To make a long story short we got busy and things got ugly and I had to put his ass out." Rachel said.

"Ha!Ha!Ha! What possessed you to fuck that man on the first date? You should've known that you didn't have a shot in hell of keeping him after that anyway. That's funny as hell! Why did you put him out? He wasn't working with anything?" Rena stated still laughing at Rachel for being so stupid.

"I was possessed by what he was packing between his legs. He had already taken his clothes off by the time I walked back into the living room from the kitchen. Shit. I haven't had any in a while and when I saw him I wanted it. It was that simple. But while we were getting busy, he yells out some other woman's name. When I called him on it he blows it off and tells me I shouldn't get mad because I had some old picture of me and Tony on the mantle. He acted like he set the shit up. He noticed the picture earlier that evening before we went out and had a little attitude about it. I thought it was over with cause we had a nice time at the club. Anyway, we had words so I put his ass out my place butt ass naked and threw his shit in the parking lot. I guess it's safe to assume that I won't be hearing from him again." Chandelle, Nia and Rena were on the couch cracking up.

"Girl that was some funny shit! You're always in something stupid behind your men. I needed a reason to smile. It took me away from my situation for a minute. Wish my situation was that easy to fix." Chandelle picked up the letter from the table and placed it and the photos inside the envelope and threw it back on the table.

"As old as we are, we shouldn't be going through this dumb shit. All of us are having issues and they all involve money or some man who isn't handling his business." Nia said reaching for a fresh beer.

"I hear you. The man problem is easy to deal with. We can dump their asses. But if we dump them then we will be hurt for cash. Except for Chandelle and Rachel but it's because of a man Chandelle is about to lose her job and Rachel swore up and down that a man was going to be the answer to her prayers and she wouldn't have to lift a finger to help her damn self." Rena said.

"I'm done depending on men. I decided to go back to school as soon as I find out how I can afford to do it. So, you can chill with the prince charming stories Rena." Rachel said rolling her eyes.

"What if I told you ladies that I had a plan that would take care of all our financial problems?" Chandelle rose from the couch and stood in the middle of the living room floor with all eyes on her.

"What are you talking about Chandelle? *I knew she was up to something. She was too damn calm after being threatened about losing her job. Rena thought to herself.*

"A couple of weeks ago a co-worker called me to her office about a program that wasn't properly. So, I went down to check it out to help her get it up and running. The problem was that an account started out with a beginning balance but after money was drawn against it for expenses, the balance still reflected the beginning balance." Chandelle paused for effect.

"Okay. And? I still don't get it. I must be missing something. The client had a beginning balance, spent for expenses and had the same beginning balance in their account. Did someone make a deposit?" Rena asked.

"No. There weren't any deposits made. So…" Rena interrupted Chandelle,

"Make a long story short. Don't nobody care or is interested in no accounting babble but you. What does this have to do with us?"

"If you'd shut the fuck up and listen, I'll tell you. I tried to work on the program and couldn't figure out why it wasn't working. So, I went ahead and created a program that would work in its place. I put the program to the side and figured it would be a pet project I'd work on later in my spare time. It wasn't until I went to the casino that it hit me. I won a couple of dollars then lost it back with everything else I had in my purse."

"I told you to stay out of that casino Chandelle. You need to go have your ass checked out at that Gamblers Anonymous place. I swear you got a problem. That's why I don't stick my money in them damn machines." Rachel said.

"No, you don't stick your money in the damn machines cause your ass is broke. But listen. I had this idea. What if I could copy the program from the accounting program onto the player's card from the casino? I could fool the casino into thinking that it isn't losing any money but in actuality we would be transferring the funds from the machine to our bank accounts." Chandelle said proud of herself.

"Bitch you crazy? You're talking about robbing a casino? You can get life for some shit like that." Rena frowned, her face convinced Chandelle has lost her mind.

"That's only if we get caught." Chandelle stated with a smirk.

"Let's be rational here. Chandelle what makes you think that something like this will work?" Nia said.

"Nia of all people, I know you aint entertaining this. You're as straight laced as they come. Plus you have those kids. You can't afford to get caught up. Besides, Chandelle ain't serious. Are you Chandelle?" Rachel said praying her friends weren't going off the deep end.

"I'm dead serious. I won't go into all the details right now. In fact I didn't think too much of it at the time. But now that I might lose my job behind some bullshit, I'm taking the possibility seriously."

Game For Fame

"Chandelle we are like sisters and I've always had your back but this is some deep shit. But I have some questions. For one, what do you need us to do? Two, when do you plan on doing this?" Rena asked.

"I don't need you to do anything. I'm just offering you a chance to get paid and not depend on some man to take care of you. I'm going to try it out and give it a trial run and iron out any potential glitches if there are any. If it goes as I planned that it will, we're about to get paid in full. Anybody hungry? " Chandelle walked towards the kitchen for another helping of chicken. Nia and Rachel sat on the couch discussing the possibility of Chandelle being able to pull off her idea. Rena ran down the hallway to talk to Chandelle in private not wanting Rachel and Nia to overhear.

"Chandelle, I hope you know what you're doing. But whatever you decide, I'm with you. When are you going to the casino? Rena wanted it to be clear that she has already made up her mind that she was willing to back her up.

"I'm going to try it out first Rena. If it works out I'll call all of you here again for a meeting to allow you to decide what you want to do. I appreciate you having my back Rena. I knew I would be able to count on you." Chandelle reached over and gave Rena a hug and kiss on her cheek.

"Let me get back in there and let the other two know that they will have to keep their mouths closed about this. That includes you too Rena. We can't afford to let this get out. It can ruin everything before we get a chance to even get started."

Y'vet

Chapter 10

Ring! Ring! You have reached the voicemail…Click! Answer your damn phone Rena! Ricky has been trying to get in touch with Rena all night. *Damn, I fell asleep and she took my shit.* He left ten voicemails asking her to call home immediately and she has yet to return any phone calls. *She left a note saying that she was going out and call if anything was needed but she doesn't answer the fucking phone. I need my keys to meet the connect. I don't trust any of these niggas and I can't take them anyway. I know something's up with Tre so he's out of the question but he'll be dealt with later.* Bam! Bam! Bam! *It's the Pittsburgh Police Department! Open Up!* "What the fuck?" Ricky ran to the bedroom to make sure the floorboards were secure and covered with the area rug. He quickly opened the closet to secure the false wall where his stash was hidden. Ricky knew that there was only one way in the apartment and one way out. Calmly Ricky left the bedroom to answer the front door.

"We are looking for Ricardo Sheldon aka Ricky Sheldon. Are you Ricky Sheldon?" The police officer stated pulling his cuffs from around his waist.

"Yeah, why?" Ricky said.

"Mr. Sheldon, you are under arrest. You have the right to remain silent. Anything you say may be held against you… Ricky never heard his Miranda rights. His thoughts were figuring out who set him up and who knew that he was meeting his connect today. The six- foot officer who was reading his rights asked if he had any sharp objects on him. Ricky nodded no, was patted down and cuffs were placed on his wrists.

"We have a warrant for your arrest and a subpoena to search the premises." Seven officers entered the small apartment and began ram shacking the place as if knowing what they were searching for. Two officers began in the living room tearing the pillows from the chairs and sofa. Each had box cutters slicing the cushions and pulling the foam interior to the floor. Each room was treated as the last. Dishes were heard hitting the floor and breaking as all the cupboards were emptied in the kitchen.

"Hey Sarge! In here! We just hit pay dirt!" Ricky watched as the officer walked to the bedroom to see what was uncovered. He held his breath hoping this was all a bad dream.

"There was a false wall in this closet. Look down here at this safe sir. We need a locksmith out here immediately. You can now get our friend out there out of here and down to central booking and get the paperwork started. We'll update you on what we find." Sergeant Bill Cooghan was leaving the room when he was called by one of the rookies.

"Hey, Sarge! This should get you those lieutenant stripes if our information was correct." Officer Cooghan smiled and said.

"Good job boys! I'll be sure to put in some recommendations for all your hard work on this one." Sergeant Cooghan called into his shoulder radio stating his location and a need for a locksmith.

"Looks like you'll be locked up for a long time scumbag." Two officers following behind the sergeant grabbed Ricky to his feet and escorted him out the house to the paddy wagon.

Rena drove home the scenic route to think about the night's events. *Nia's man left her for some young chick, giving up the goods on the first date played Rachel and Chandelle is trippin' and talking about robbing a bank. I got to get home and talk to Ricky. I took his keys to make sure he can't go anywhere till I get there and he's been blowing up my phone and I missed his calls. Now he's not answering his calls. He's going to have a fucking fit when I get home. But we need to talk just not tonight. After being with my girls, I have to do this differently than I had planned. Maybe I'll get lucky and he called one of his boys and went out.* Rena pulled up to her apartment complex and saw an unusually large amount of people standing around for one o'clock in the morning. She pulled up into her reserved parking space and exited her car. As she walked towards her apartment everyone's eyes seemed to be on her. Ms. Saunders from next door peeked her head out from her door and spoke.

"Hey Rena honey, you all right?" Ms. Saunders wrapped her robbed tightly around her round waist and stepped outside her door

"Yes mam. Why you ask? Rena asked staring at her neighbor with concern.

"There was some police at your apartment earlier tonight and they took your friend outta there in handcuffs. I just figured you knew what happened and I wanted to make sure you were okay." Ms. Saunders being nosey and reporting everybody's business walked towards Rena backing her closer to her door so she could get a peek inside.

"Uh, yeah. I'm okay Ms. Saunders. Thank you for your concern." Rena walked towards Ms. Saunders to avoid her entering her apartment. Rena knew she was going to have to perform damage control fast. Thinking quick on her feet she said,

"I have to go down to the police department in the morning to check on my friend. From what I understand he was arrested on a false identification charge. I'm going to take his license down in the morning after he sees the judge." Rena raced toward her apartment and tore the notice down that was taped to her front door. Once inside she held back a scream from the chaos inside. She fell to her knees with her hands on her face and cried for what seemed like hours. Pulling herself together she saw that her living room was in shambles and her kitchen and bedroom were equally destroyed. Rena walked back to the living room and sat on the floor to read the noticed that was tacked to her front door.

Ms. Charles,

Y'vet

You are hereby informed that eviction procedures have been filed against you. Article 12 of your lease states that if for any reason the police or any other authorized agency gains entry into any dwelling for illegal activities against the lease holder or guests there of, the lessee will be evicted within thirty days of notice

Charles Benson,

Property Manager.

Stanwick Properties

Oh My God Ricky!! What the fuck did you do? I know you didn't have any shit up in my house!!! Rena dropped the notice to the floor while a fresh set of tears flowed down her face.

Chapter 11

"Mommy! Daddy is on the phone!" Melanie dropped the phone on the kitchen counter and ran to the living room to finish watching cartoons before heading off to church.

"Good morning Tyrik. What can I do for you and hurry up cause church starts in a half hour." Nia turned her back away from the living room so her daughter couldn't overhear her conversation with her father.

"Good morning to you too Nia. I just called to let you know that I figured you would be in church this morning so I wanted to stop by the house and pick up some more clothes."

Why Tyrik? We can't sit down and talk face to face anymore? I take it you must have come to a decision if you're picking up clothes. You're leaving for good without plans on coming back? Is that it? You might as well tell me now. There's no need in hiding it if that's what you want to do." Nia's voice was raising an octave with each word that passed her lips. She was angry but hurt that her marriage has completely broken down and she may have lost her husband.

"I didn't say I was leaving for good Nia. I just said I wanted to come and get more clothes. I need more time to think that's all."

"More time to think? Think about what? How the hell are you going to make a decision without me? There's no revolving door here ass hole! In fact you don't ever have to come back! I don't need your raggedy cheatin ass." Nia said checking over her shoulder to monitor how much her daughter may have overheard.

"Hold on." Nia placed the phone on her shoulder to muffle the sound to keep Tyrik from realizing that their daughter may have overheard.

"Melanie sweetheart, go upstairs and finish getting dressed for church. I'll be up there in a minute to get you and your sister." She watched as her daughter turned off the television and climbed the stairs.

"Look Tyrik. Right through here I don't care what you do. You can stay out there and move in with your bitch if you want to. I don't need you."

"I don't know what has gotten into you lately Nia. I don't know you anymore. Listen to the way you're talking to me. The woman I married never talked like that. She was always optimistic and didn't have a mouth from the gutter. And you're on your way to church? You need to stay away from those so-called friends of yours. I think they are the reason why you act like a fool. Furthermore, I never said that you needed me. But you need to check yourself. You can't take care of a house, two kids, and all the bills you accumulated. So, you need to be a little more understanding and give me what I asked for. My responsibility is those kids only and if you can't take care of my girls, I'll be happy to take them. So, if you want to continue to live comfortably…

"Fuck you Tyrik!" *click.* Nia didn't give Tyrik a chance to continue his I'm doing you a favor speech. *I don't know why he thinks I'm desperate and I need him.* Nia said aloud. *I'm calling Chandelle tonight. Dear Lord help me…*

Chandelle pulled out of her garage headed towards the electronics store to pick up some materials needed to put her plan in place. She didn't notice that parked across the street was a black Charger with tinted windows. As she pulled onto the highway headed east the car eased into traffic trailing two cars behind her. Chandelle drove two blocks and got off at the next exit where Electronic Depot was located in the shopping center on the left. Chandelle parked and walked to the store to browse the selections. Five minutes later the owner of the Charger entered the store and watched as Chandelle talked to a store clerk.

Game For Fame

"Thank you so much for your help. I'm sure everything here will work just fine." Chandelle thanked the clerk gathered her purchases and turned to walk towards the checkout when she noticed the woman blocking her way.

"Did you get my letter? Angela stood in front of Chandelle with a smile on her face.

"I have the advantage here don't I? Your arms are full and I could kick your ass up in here." Angela walked closer getting into Chandelle's face.

"Back up out my space you crazy bitch. You put your hands on me and you're gonna get what you came in here for." Chandelle darted her eyes left and right searching for a place to drop her purchases and make space between her Angela.

"Angela, I'm not trying to go to jail over your craziness. I suggest you call Derek and settle whatever issues the two you may have. But I'm not our problem."

"Oh you *are* the problem. Stay away from my husband and I'm not going to tell you again. I let your boss know you're a hoe and don't care who knows it. Thanks to those pictures and the note I dropped inside the package with them." Chandelle dropped what she was holding and lounged for Angela's throat. Angela ducked left and stepped backwards.

"Don't get stupid bitch. This time I only stepped to your boss but next time you won't be so lucky and I'm coming for you. Trust there will be a next time. You better watch your back." Angela turned away before the store security was able to approach them to see about the disturbance and walked out the front door. Chandelle followed behind Angela only to see her releasing the alarm on her Charger and starting the car to pull off.

Chandelle walked back into the store paid for her purchases and grabbed her cell phone from her purse. Once again she and Derek were playing phone tag. She left a message telling him to get to her house immediately.

Ricky was seated in a quiet room at central booking waiting to be interrogated by the arresting officers. The procedure wasn't new to Ricky because he was arrested a year before on a misdemeanor aggravated assault charge. He broke the arm and leg of one of the dealers from the east side. He was brought in and interrogated by the police hoping that he would turn evidence on the boss from the east side. Ricky was able to plead down his charges because his rival never made it to court but there were enough witnesses to testify against him that he could still do some jail time. His lawyer spoke to the prosecutor getting his charges reduced. Ricky spent Saturday night in the bull- pen he figured the officers wanted him to sweat what he was being charged with. Two detectives walked in the room one standing against the wall while the other pulled up a chair opposite of Ricky. *Here we go with the good cop bad cop shit.* Ricky thought to himself.

"Good Evening Mr. Sheldon. I'm detective York. Do you know why you have been arrested Mr. Sheldon? Ricky shook his head no but remained close mouthed. He hadn't planned on answering any questions without his lawyer present but knew it was unlikely that he would be able to contact him until Monday. He figured he would kill some time and get out from around the hard legs and find out what he was being charged with.

"You're being charged with tax evasion Fifty thousand dollars was found in a safe at your residence. We suspect that you're involved with dealing drugs and were about to become a major player Mr. Sheldon. Do you mind if I call you Ricky? I hate to think that we have to be so formal around here." Ricky shrugged and nodded yes not caring either way. Detective York continued,

"Now Ricky we've been keeping an eye on you and our informants on the street dropped a dime on you that you were to meet your connect tonight. Can you confirm any of this for us?" Ricky continued to stare at detective York remaining silent while his partner walked towards the table. York raised his hand indicating to his partner to back away from the table cause he had things under control. York chuckled and smoothed his hand over his hair.

"I didn't expect you to speak up right away but since you have been cooperating and agreed to come to the table without counsel, we have decided to cut you a deal if you agree to give us what we are looking for now. Give us the information on your connect. We know it's Jimmy James from New York and you've been in negotiations with James and can be confirmed. Two of his boys have been intercepted on their way to Pittsburgh and told us about your connection to James. They are willing to testify against you in court for prior drug transactions in a deal to keep them out of jail. So, out the goodness of my heart I can speak to the DA to offer you the same deal. We just need you to set up a meeting, make the exchange and you could be looking at five to ten instead of twenty-five to life. What do you think Ricky? Ricky looked at detective York then turned around and glanced at his partner. Crossing his legs and folding his hands together and putting them on his lap Ricky said,

"I don't know what you're talking about. I need to see my lawyer and I'd like to make my phone call now." York rose from the table and called to his partner.

"Cuff him and take him back to his cell. Ricky I want you to know that refusing to talk to us all deals are off the table." Ricky was removed and taken back to population.

Derek was doing seventy in a fifty-five mile an hour zone racing to get to Chandelles house. He received her message and called her to find out what was so important. But there had been no answer. He checked his voicemails but there were no messages. There was a text from her number though from her number repeating her urgency. And there was the page. He wondered why she had paged him using 911. She hardly if

74

ever paged him and never used 911. He never bothered to call her. If Chandelle needed him there was no question that he would be there for her. Derek pulled up and parked. He quickly jumped out his car and ran to her door and rang the bell. Chandelle opened her door and upon seeing Derek in the doorway slapped him across his face. Derek stood in the doorway and grabbed his jaw in a state of shock.

"Chandelle what did you hit me for? What did I do?"

'You're lucky that all I did was slap you. I wanted to get a knife and cut your ass. I told you to handle your business!" Chandelle walked away from the door allowing Derek to enter.

"What the fuck you talking about Chandelle?" Derek entered the house closing the door behind him.

"This is what I'm talking about Derek!" Chandelle threw the envelope at Derek and watched as he picked up the envelope removing its contents. Derek stood in silence skimming through the pictures.

"What the hell is that Derek? Your boss's wife? You're a dog and I'm through with your trifling ass! You're a liar and a cheat and I want you to handle that bitch before I do. How the fuck are you going to photograph you and I in bed and not tell me!" Chandelle walked towards Derek to smack him again. Derek grabbed her arm before impact.

"Chandelle let me explain. That picture with my boss's wife and me was taken a long time ago. I just graduated from college and I met her when I applied for my job at the marketing firm. She came on to me and we had a short fling. It wasn't until after we slept together that I found out who she was. I hired shortly after that. We called things off and she moved on to the next man. She claims that they have an open relationship and swore her husband would never find out. She has kept her word. I never thought anyone would find out. I don't know where the pictures came from. I suspect that Angela has planted a camera in my bedroom. I never took those pictures of you and me. She was in my apartment twice. Once when I first moved in and she brought the movers there when I left the house. The other time was when she brought our daughter to the house so that I could spend time with her. She went off then asking if I was seeing someone then. That's when she probably planted the camera. I don't know Chandelle. She's crazy. I told you that before from some of the antics she pulled in the past." Chandelle calmed down slightly and he released her arm from his grip.

"Read the letter. I ran into her earlier today at the electronics store. She followed me there and approached me in the store. She let me know that she has already sent those pictures to my job addressed to my boss. There's no doubt I'm going to lose my job behind this. I am in contact with important clients. There is no way I'd be able to continue to work there with a risk of something like this getting out. She said that she would be back in touch with me and I believe her." Chandelle walked towards her window and pulled back the curtains looking up and down the street for any sign of Angela's car. She turned around and faced Derek and continued,

"You should've seen the look on her face. That bitch needs to be committed. You need to get your daughter from her if you care about her at all. You can't want that bitch raising her. But you know what? You won't have to worry about her cause if she steps to me again I'm takin her ass out of here. I mean that shit too Derek. I can't be watching my back every five minutes wondering if she is going to sneak me." Derek walked towards Chandelle but she back away from his embrace.

"Chandelle I'm sorry. I'm going to leave here and go to her house and put an end to this right now. If I have to give her what she is asking for in the divorce decree then I will. I'll fix this baby, I swear. I'm sorry about your job but I'll pay your bills until you are able to get back on your feet. Just tell me that you are not going to throw away what we have. Give me some time to handle this." Derek grabbed Chandelle's hands and looked in her eyes praying that she would reconsider.

"I don't think so Derek. I have some things that I have to take care of and I can't be distracted by you, Angela or anything else. I'll be in touch." Chandelle walked to the door and opened it for Derek to leave. Slowly he walked towards the door.

"Please Chandelle reconsider. I love you. I'm not giving up this easily. I'll call you after I take care of Angela." Chandelle didn't answer and closed the door behind him.

Chapter 12

Putting her relationship out of her mind was the first priority for Chandelle. There wasn't going to be anything that was going to be more important than going through with her plans. *I can't deal with Derek and his baggage right now. If we weren't meant to be than so be it. I'm tired. Just tired and that wife of his is crazy. It's time to move on and I have a plan to do it. Fuck it. I'm going for it. What did Erykah Badu say? I guess I'll see you next lifetime.* Chandelle sang aloud. *I need a plan on moving out of here and a place to go. If this works out like planned, I'm going to need to move up out of Pittsburgh. Maybe I'll move out west somewhere. I got to remember to call off work in the morning cause this is going to be a long night. I might as well get started now. Chandelle's phone rang interrupting her thoughts.* Walking towards the phone she answered hoping it wasn't Derek because she didn't want to get into an argument at that moment.

"Hello?"

"Hey Chandelle it's me Nia."

"What's going on Nia?" Chandelle asked gathering her laptop from the living room table headed towards her bedroom.

"I made a decision. I want in on your venture. I thought about it since you mentioned it on Saturday and I'm sure this is what I want to do."

"Nia I told you guys about my plan and I didn't really think it through. It was only this morning that I went out and bought a few things and saw this as being a possibility. It wasn't until I heard everything that was going on with all of us that I got frustrated and said anything about it. What I'm trying to say is that before you get yourself involved, I need to see if it's going to work." Chandelle said cautioning her friend.

Y'vet

"I heard you when you said you were going to try it out first. I just wanted you to know that if it works out, I'm in on the second run." Chandelle heard the desperation in Nia's voice.

"Did something happen since we talked last night Nia? You seem awfully sure about this. It's just not like you. You have more to lose than any of us. You have kids and a husband. I don't even think this would be a possibility if I had that kind of responsibility."

"I don't think Tyrik is coming back. He came by today while me and the kids were at church and picked up some more of his things. I spoke with him on the phone and I lost it. He more or less told me that I need to let him do his thing and when he was ready to decide what he was going to do he'd let me know. It was like you take my shit until I'm done playing then maybe I'll come home." Nia said beginning to get upset again.

"What? No he didn't girl! Are you sure that's what he meant or are you just upset and haven't thought things through. I know I wasn't much support last night but you know what I'm going through with Derek. It got in the way because I was being a little selfish. But your case is different. You love your husband and I'm sure he loves you. You need to both cool off and give yourselves some space and talk about things when you both had time to think." Chandelles thought about Derek and wondered if she was being hasty in throwing away her relationship or should she be supportive and see him through his divorce. After all he was trying to get a divorce. She quickly dismissed the idea cause her problems were so much deeper than that.

"I don't think so. He threw in my face the fact that I don't have any money and how I needed him to take care of the kids and me so I didn't have any choice in the matter concerning what he did. He's out of his mind if he thinks that because he takes care of the majority of the bills around here that I need him. I don't need his ass. Granted I could get a job and suffer a little till I get on my feet but I would probably have to move into a small apartment until that happened. I don't want to uproot these kids Chandelle. Your plan would allow me to continue to live as I've been living and I could put a couple of dollars in the bank till I found a job."

"I hear you Nia but…" Chandelle began to say but was interrupted.

"Do you know he told me that he would take the girls from me?" Nia said.

"Wow, Nia. He *is* trippin'. I'm so sorry this is happening to you. Well, I'm going through with this and I'm trying it out in a couple of days or so. I'll let you girls know what happened and we can make plans from there." Chandelle looked at her clock and noticed the time wanting to get started on her project.

"Look Nia. Let me go. If you need anything let me know. I'm here for you. But I gotta go and get started. I'll talk to you later. Chandelle waited till Nia said her goodbyes and hung up the phone. Gathering her bag from Electronics Depot and her laptop, Chandelle headed for the steps leading to her bedroom when her doorbell rang. *Who the fuck is it now? I'm never going to get anything done!* Placing her things down on the floor, Chandelle walked towards her door and looked out the peephole. Rena was standing on the doorstep looking distraught wiping tears from her face trying unsuccessfully to pull herself together before Chandelle opened the door.

"Rena what's wrong girl? Get in here." Chandelle reached for Rena's arm and pulled her inside. She hardly recognized the woman standing in front of her. Rena was always put together but tonight her designer sundress was wrinkled on the bottom probably from sitting crossed legged on the floor. Her eyes were puffy and red from seemingly hours of crying and her hair lost its curl from being combed straight back instead of its bouncy full bob style she wore effortlessly.

"Everything." Rena said with her lips trembling ready to break down into tears. Trying to pull herself together she continued,

"When I got home last night…or should I say this morning, my house was ram shacked by the police and they took Ricky to jail."

"What? Come sit down and tell me what happened." Chandelle led Rena to the couch while she took a seat beside her.

Y'vet

"Do you want me to get you something to drink?" Chandelle asked?

"No. Thanks I'll be okay." Rena pulled a tissue from her purse and wiped her tears. She then took a deep breath and got her thoughts together to explain what happened.

"When I pulled up to my complex, my neighbor Ms. Saunders told me that the police were at my house and arrested Ricky. When I got in my apartment I figured out that they were looking for drugs because my house was tore up. They tore up the whole house girl. The police tore up all the cushions on my couch and my chairs. The pictures were torn off my walls and the vases and books on my shelves were all turned over on the floor and broken. My kitchen glasses and plates were pulled out of the cupboards and shattered on the floor. The drawers were pulled out with forks and knives on the floor. Even the oven door was open with the racks pulled out as if there was a secret door in the oven or some shit like that. My bathroom was torn up. You should have seen my bedroom... Rena was talking so fast Chandelle stopped her so she could take a breath.

"Calm down some Rena. Those are just things. They can be replaced. It's going to be all right." Chandelle grabbed her friend's hands and squeezed them tightly reassuring her that everything was going to be all right.

"My bedroom was the worse. The mattress was against the wall with the stuffing all over the room. All of our clothes were everywhere. They pulled everything from the racks and shelves. My perfume was broken on the floor and jewelry was strewn across the dresser. There wasn't anything left in my dresser drawers. It doesn't make any sense for them to tear up my room like that. What did they expect to find in a perfume bottle? They didn't have to break my shit up like that." Rena held her head as if a headache was coming on.

"Rena. Listen to me. Take your hands off your face and look at me." Chandelle pulled her hands down and gently leaned Rena back against the pillows on the couch.

81

"Pull yourself together. We have to find out what's going on. Did you call the police department?"

"Yeah. They said that Ricky has been arrested but he hasn't been arraigned yet so there isn't any bail so I don't know what he is being held for." Rena said.

"Chandelle that's not my only problem. There was a note on my door from my landlord that said I had thirty days to leave the premises. Somebody must have notified my landlord when they saw the police." Rena got up from the couch and began pacing the floor.

"Not necessarily Rena. The police may have notified the landlord so they can gain entry to the apartment if nobody was there. You said the place was a wreck so they had to have a warrant and subpoena to check the apartment. If they took Ricky they must have found something unless he had a prior warrant. Did you have his name on the lease? Chandelle asked.

"Yes. I put his name on the lease after I found out he was making some moves. I never thought that the police would run up in my place but I just didn't want to be blamed for anything in the apartment that wasn't mine. I ain't that stupid. He said he didn't have anything in the apartment but something told me to cover my ass. You know he was happy about signing cause in his mind he thought that we were going to stay together. I could've covered the rent once I broke up with him so I wasn't going to sue him. That is until I lost my job. Then I was glad that I did it. His ass would've been liable for half of the rent." Rena walked towards the kitchen in search for a beer.

"Okay that was good. That's probably why the police weren't still at the apartment waiting to arrest you. So we can assume that they found what they were looking for and arrested Ricky." Chandelle waited for Rena to take a seat with her beer assuring she had her undivided attention. "Tomorrow you are going to have to get down to the court for his arraignment. Even if you don't have the money for his bail, he may have it or he may even have a lawyer on retainer. But most importantly,

Y'vet

you need to find out what he's talking. Get yourself on his visitors list if he hasn't done it already. You can't afford to have him down at that jail flippin' the script blaming you for whatever the cops found in there." Rena shook her head.

"I didn't even think of that. He better not get his ass down there talking about his shit belonged to me. I don't want to go back there tonight. Can I stay here for the night? Rena took a sip from her beer bottle then placed on the table in front of her.

"You know you don't have to ask to stay here. I'm going to go get the spare bedroom ready for you. You can stay down here and relax and come up whenever you're ready. I need to get started on that project we talked about last night. By the way, Nia called me an hour ago and she said that she is definitely in."

"What?!" Rena said shocked.

"Yep, she's in. I'll tell you about it later when you come up." Chandelle headed towards the stairs retrieving her things on the way.

Game For Fame

Chapter 13

Chandelle woke up early Monday morning making sure she called in to take a few days off. She didn't want to speak directly with her boss and left a message with his assistant that she wouldn't be in. The first item on her agenda was double-checking that she had her program ready for the big test. She stayed up till two in the morning writing the program. Chandelle turned on her laptop, checked the program for accuracy and placed the disc in her laptop case. All she had to do was transfer the program to her players' card she'd received from the casino for the plan to work. Her next stop was Electronics Depot where for twenty-nine ninety-five, they can transfer written programs from a disc onto metallic strips for personal use. Her plan was to transfer the strip to the back of her players' card once she returned home. The service was originally designed for amateur programmers trying to patent their ideas and have them sold to major software companies. One of the local high schools held a science fair the year before and the winning entry was from a student who wrote an electronic game and later sold it to EA Sports for a million dollars for their Xbox System. Next she had to get to the bank. She had a connection already set up with the bank to track her winnings and losses at the casino for tax purposes. Because she didn't plan on losing she needed to set up an account where she would be able to have money deposited into her checking account without raising any red flags. Her first run was to go into the casino and get just enough money to make sure her plan would work. Later she would set up an off shore account to protect her money. She just needed to decide where and how much she planned on taking from the casino. Her research on banks recommended that anything over two hundred thousand she would need to wire her funds to Switzerland or Luxemburg. In that case, she would have to send the money over to the accounts in increments so there wouldn't be any questions asked or accused of money laundering. Anything fewer than two hundred thousand she could send to the

Caymans without any risks involved. *I pray that having to decide where to put my money is the only problem I have. That would mean I'm paid in full. I can't believe that I'm doing this but I'm tired of the bullshit and I want to start my life over on my own terms. Shit, if I want to I can start up my own software firm if I want to. Let me go check on Rena and get out of here.* Chandelle walked down the hall and knocked on the bedroom door.

"Rena, are you up?" Chandelle knocked again.

"Yeah, come in. I'm getting dressed getting ready to go down to the courthouse. Arraignments start at nine. I guess I'll have to wait through all the cases until Ricky's comes up. I can either post his bail if I can or at least get in a visit later in the afternoon. Either way he'll know that I'm there to support him." Chandelle came into the room and sat down on the bed next to Rena.

"I wish I could be there with you. I know you're scared and need my support but just be strong and hang in there. You have to protect yourself girl and find out where his head is. Make sure you call me and let me know what's going on." Chandelle got up from the bed after checking her watch and noticed that it was after eight. She wanted to be at the bank when it opened and didn't want to hold Rena up causing her to be late.

"It's late. Get going before you're late. Don't forget to call me."

"Alright girl, I'll be fine. I'll talk to you later." Chandelle left her room and headed towards the front door.

"Rachel got off the bus at Fifth and Smithfield headed towards the employee entrance at Macy's. The store was due to open in a half hour which gave Rachel plenty of time to ride the elevator to the fifth floor employee lounge and grab a cup of coffee before heading to the Fashion Fair makeup counter she was assigned to that day. Rachel walked passed the lockers into the lounge where she seen a couple of her co-workers already having coffee engrossed in conversation. Kelly and Deanne were known for hanging out on the regular. They were both ambitious and wanted to become heads of their departments. Kelly worked in the boys department. She was head cashier and trained all the new employees in her department but she wanted to be in charge of the new designs and lay out of the kids' floor. She put in extra hours before and after her regular schedule shadowing the current buyer to learn the job. She had been passed up two times before when the job was up for bid. Deanne worked in the jewelry department and believed her good looks were going to get her promoted.

"Good morning ladies. What's going on?" Rachel grabbed her coffee and took a seat at the table.

"We were just talking about the notice that human resources put out this morning over there on the bulletin board." Kelly said pointing towards the bulletin board.

"I didn't see it. What does it say?" Rachel said sipping her coffee.

"It outlines the changes human resources made for employees who wish to apply for future openings at the store. It states that any employee applying for a managerial or administrative position must have a four-year degree. They're no longer excepting experience alone for consideration for a promotion." Deanne said.

"That's bullshit. I've been working my ass off around here trying to prove myself and get a promotion. I worked here for seven years and been turned down two times already applying for the buyers position for the kids department." Kelly said pissed.

"Well they did state that they have a tuition matching policy which they didn't have before. So that's a good thing." Deanna said in Macy's defense.

"Well ladies you know what this is about don't you?" Rachel said and both ladies shook their heads no.

"They're weeding out people from applying for positions. That's what they're doing. No offense Kelly but you applied twice and got turned down. You then never gave up but continued to put in the extra hours and learned whatever you could from their buyer. I don't think they have any plans on hiring you for whatever their reason may be. If the job comes up again and you apply with all the experience and time you put in it they would probably turn you down again." Kelly wanted to interrupt but changed her mind.

"The problem would be what kind of repercussions or reason would Macy's give for not hiring you after your applying for a third time. They'd probably worry about a lawsuit. You're good enough to work in the department now so if you're doing such a horrible job why do they keep you? I'm not saying it's because you're black necessarily but by changing the rules you'd need a degree so you would have to go back to school. It's not just you though. It's going to take a lot of us out the running for a promotion and they know it. Now they can get fresh meat without hiring within. And if we were serious they would know it 'cause we would go to school and get that paper." Rachel walked towards the buffet to refresh her coffee.

"I hear you Rachel but its still bullshit. They are willing to pay for school if the employees put the money up first then pass the class with a C. Who the hell on our salary can afford to go to college and pay up front? They are more or less telling us to quit and take our experience elsewhere or be satisfied with job you have. I'm grateful to have a nine to five but damn what's wrong with trying to better myself?" Kelly said.

"Lower your voices ladies before we're out of a job by the end of the day. I'm as ambitious as the next person but it is what it is. If I want this bad enough I guess I'm going to have to consider going to school." Deanna said.

"Well, that's easy for you to say cause you have a rich boyfriend who can pay your way to school if you decide that's what you want to do. I'm not hatin' but I don't have that option." Rachel thought about her own situation. She was older than her co-workers and knew that at thirty-five if school was going to be a possibility, she needed to make a decision now. She still had hopes of getting married and having children of her own but she wasn't twenty anymore and her pickins' were slim in the men department. Forty was pushing it for considering having children if she enrolled the next fall semester and graduated on time. *I wasn't trying to make a career out of working at Macy's but this certainly makes me look at my options. This shit is just slapping me in the face all at once. Maybe everything that is going on in my life is happening for a reason. John, school...I don't know about robbing a casino but the possibility is certainly tempting.*

Derek called Angela on the house phone and waited for her to answer. After she picked up and said hello he hung up the phone. He wanted only to be sure that she would be there when he got to the house. He knew his daughter was at school so he wouldn't have any interruptions when he confronted Angela. Derek used his key to open the door on the side entrance. He wanted to be sure that Angela wouldn't shut the door on him and not allow him entry to the house. After entering and searching through the bottom floor he figured she hadn't come down stairs yet because the coffee pot hadn't been turned on in the kitchen. Derek walked towards the stairs and called for her to come downstairs.

"Angela! Come downstairs now! We need to talk!" Derek yelled.

"Derek is that you? How the fuck are you just going to walk in my house? You don't live here anymore and I don't want to talk to you." Angela yelled without going to the top of the stairs.

"Get your ass down here now. You don't want me to come up there and get you!"

"Get the fuck out Derek before I call police! " Derek took the steps two at a time reaching the bedroom door watching Angela give herself a pedicure.

"Angela. What the fuck do you think you're doing following Chandelle and threatening her? Have you lost your fucking mind?"

Derek walked towards the phone on the nightstand not to risk Angela trying to make good on her threat of calling the police. She closed the nail polish bottle tightly then leaned back against the pillows and laughed.

"Ha! Ha! Ha! What happened? Your bitch calls you for protection? She's lucky I didn't kick her ass up in that store. I'm not going to have you make a fool out of me out there in the streets Derek. Call her and tell her that your little fling is over." Angela got off the bed and walked towards Derek.

"You know you still love me. It's time for you to come home now." Angela said as she sat back down on the bed and began blowing her toes dry.

"It's over Angela. I don't want you anymore. Your threatening Chandelle and the pictures you have of me are not going to work. When are you going to get that through your head? You can't make somebody stay if they don't want to. I've had enough of your games. You wasted enough of my time. You're not going to get more." Derek said growing angrier. Angela jumped from the bed and into Derek's face.

"Wasted your time? Is that what I did Derek wasted your time? Motherfucker I was with you while your ass was broke, struggling through school and had your child. I had a choice of any nigga I wanted and chose to stay with you when you wasn't shit! You got the best of my years so don't talk to me about wasting your time." Angela said spitting in his face as she spoke.

"But I tell you what. I'm gonna have a whole lot more of your time motherfucker cause your ass ain't going nowhere. I'll take you and your bitch down and you won't have shit if you don't bring your ass home." Angela mugged Derek in the forehead causing him to stumble backward. Derek caught his footing and grabbed Angela by the neck and said,

90

Y'vet

"This is the last time I'm warning you Angela, leave Chandelle alone. You and I are going to go to court and you're going to sign those divorce papers like a good girl and stay the fuck out of my life. Do you understand?" Derek released Angela pushing her backwards onto the bed. Angela rubbed her neck and shouted at Derek,

"Or what Derek? What the fuck you gonna do? I have the pictures remember that. I already sent them to your girlfriend's boss and your boss will be next if you don't come home." She said inching towards the headboard away from his reach.

"Don't let me come back here for you to find out. I'll be filing a motion for custody of our daughter too. You cut your own throat by sending those pictures. After the judge sees what kind of woman you are, there is no way he'll allow you to have custody let alone think you are capable of raising our daughter. You may be lucky to be granted supervised visits." Derek turned to walk out the door when Angela took a nail file and stabbed him in the neck. Screaming Derek pulled the file from his neck and used his other hand to try to stop the bleeding protruding from the gash. Angela quickly pushed by Derek getting out the door and down the steps.

He thinks he's going to walk out on me then take my daughter and live happily ever after with his bitch? He's the one that's crazy not me. I'll be damned if he walks out on me and leaves me broke and dependent on a alimony check that I'm supposed to support myself with every month. I ain't been working and I'm not going to start now. Fuck that! We'll see who gets what. I told him don't fuck with me. I told him. I told him. I told him. She said to herself not sure if she said it out loud. Angela grabbed her purse and keys from the hallway table and ran to her car speeding off down the street.

Chandelle walked into First Union National and took a seat to wait for the next available bank representative. She browsed some of the brochures from the rack advertising the services offered by the bank.

91

After waiting five minutes a tall stately gentlemen in his mid-fifties approached her offering a firm handshake.

"Good morning. I'm Dan Irving one of the Vice Presidents here at First Union. How can I assist you today?" Chandelle smiled and shook his hand.

"Hi. I'm Chandelle Carter. I'd like to make some updates to my account please."

"Sure Ms. Carter. I'm sure I can help you with that today. Allow me to lead you to my office. This way please." Mr. Irving waved Chandelle to step in front of him allowing her to lead the way.

"It's the next office on the right. Please go in and make yourself comfortable." Chandelle took the seat in front of the mahogany desk while the bank officer made his way to his matching burgundy leather chair.

"So, Ms Carter you stated that you would like to make some changes to your account. What exactly can I help you with today? Mr. Irving waited while Chandelle searched through her purse for her identification, checkbook, and bankcard.

"I would like my account set up so that I can track how much money I've won and lost at the *River's Edge* casino. Chandelle passed her information to the bank representative so that he could access her information on the computer.

"Well, I hope we will be tracking more winnings than losses Ms. Carter." He said smiling. After locating her information he stated,

"Okay, I have your information right here. I believe I can help you with that but there are couple things I need to explain. What we do here at the bank is track money spent and earned at the casino for tax purposes. I know you understand that because that is the reason you are here. However, you will not be able to take money directly from your bankcard and gamble directly into the machines. Many customers

92

believe that they can connect their player's cards and bankcards together for easy access to their checking accounts without using the ATM machines. You will need to withdraw money from the ATM if you wish to gamble. So, you can only use funds that are available in your checking account." Do you understand what I just explained to you Ms. Carter?" Chandelle shook her head yes.

"I believe so. So how will the bank track how much money I spent if my ATM card isn't connected to the player's card?" Chandelle asked.

"What you will need to do is decide how much money you would like to spend and take that amount along with the player's card to the cashier's window and they will put that amount on your account. That money would then be available on the players' card so that you can play the slots until you either increase your balance because you are on a winning streak or you deplete your balance. You then have the option of withdrawing more money and starting the process all over again. It's a headache to continue to walk back and forth to the cashier to deposit money to your account but you have to set a limit for yourself and stick with it so that you don't overdraw your checking account or spend more money than you planned." Chandelle shook her head again indicating she understood. Mr. Irving continued.

"Now, if by the end of the evening you have any money left on your players' card, you will be able to electronically transfer those funds back into your checking account." Chandelle raised her left eyebrow in question.

"That just doesn't make sense that you can deposit money back into the checking account but can't take it out." Mr. Irving agreed.

"Yes, it does sound strange. But you have to understand that the bank wants your business so we do this as a courtesy. The casino wants your money so they want you to withdraw from the ATM machines and put the money on the players' cards. Once money goes on the card they figure the likelihood of it going into the slot machines is highly probable. They are in the business of making money. At the end of the year, the bank will send you a form that will outline all money spent and earned at the casino that you can give to your tax representative." Chandelle smiled realizing her plan would work perfectly.

"How soon after I leave the casino would my money become available? Chandelle asked.

"Oh it can be available immediately if you have access to a computer and online banking. Once you're through gambling, go to the cashier at the end of the night so they can swipe your player's card releasing the funds then you can transfer the money from the card back to your checking account online. You will be able to check your balance online, withdraw the funds from an ATM or move your money to a savings account or something similar." *Yes! Once I program my players' card to steal money from the casino my ass will be home transferring that money to my off shore account faster than a blink of an eye.*

"Ms. Carter? Ms. Carter?" Chandelle looked at Mr. Irving startled that he was calling her name and she wasn't paying attention because of her daydreaming.

"Oh. I'm sorry Mr. Irving. I was just thinking about what you said. I'll have to be careful not to spend more than I planned when I go to the casino. You are right about one thing. They are interested in making money and the odds are stacked against me. So, what else where you saying?" She fully gave him her attention.

"I was just going to say that you will need to sign some of these forms once they come off the printer. But while we are waiting for them to print, can I interest you in some of our low rate credit cards or money market accounts. The bank is giving great rates along with low finance charges."

"No, thank you. Not at this time. I will take some information home with me so that I may look it over at my leisure. However, I do have another request. I brought information with me outlining my 401k account that I have contributed to through my employer." Chandelle laid the information out for Mr. Irving to review.

"Oh this is great. You're interested in one of our IRA accounts?" He said still perusing the documents laid before him.

"No. What I'd like to do is cash in my 401k and deposit the funds into my checking account." Chandelle said.

"Ms. Carter, you do understand that cashing in your 401k without rolling the funds over will cause you to lose some of the money you have accrued and cost you a penalty that you will have to pay the IRS at the end of the year don't you? The money you have saved was non-taxable income and the IRS is going to want their share. You have a very sizable amount here. Are you sure this is something that you want to do?" Mr. Irving asked.

"Yes. Please. I have plans on investing the money shortly. I was told that I have a grace period and I hope to have the money invested before I have to pay the penalties. But thank you for your concern." Mr. Irving gathered the information needed to transfer the funds to her account.

"These funds should clear your account in a day or two. You can call the bank for its availability or check online for your balance. Is there anything else I can help you with today?" Chandelle gathered her things and placed them back in her bag.

"No. Thank you so much for your time Mr. Irving. It has been a pleasure talking with you today." Mr. Irving rose from his chair and shook Chandelle's hand as she headed towards the door.

Game For Fame

Chapter 14

Rena sat in the third row of the crowded courtroom watching as the judge handed down harsh prison sentences as the prisoners were brought in one after another like a herd of cattle. Judge Millner had a reputation of being a hard case and it was known that if you were arrested you prayed that you didn't go in front of him because chances were that you were going to do some time. Blacks believed him to be racist but at re-election time he was elected by a landslide and was congratulated that he was one of the main reasons that crime in Pittsburgh was below the national average due in large part to his hard-nosed approach to the law and no-nonsense prison sentences. Rena learned from a woman sitting next to her that the crowd in the courtroom was due to a boy arrested over the weekend because of a domestic dispute. The young man was brought in and the courtroom fell to a silence waiting to hear the charges read and the outcome. The only sounds heard were between the public defender and the assistant DA arguing the case. After five minutes of explaining the circumstances to the judge, the courtroom went into an uproar as the judge ruled that a fifteen year old being held on a murder one charge was to be held without bail and remanded and tried as an adult. He was being accused of stabbing his stepfather after an argument when the stepfather allegedly punched his mother in the face breaking her jaw after she fell onto the kitchen floor. The young man's lawyer was claiming self defense for the child but the judge stated that the authorities should have been called and there was a history of animosity between the defendant and the man in question. It seemed that the youngster was arrested twice before for domestic incidences between the two. The stepfather had asked that the boy be removed from the home. Family members were shouting racism and self-defense as the judge banged his gavel asking that the family be removed from his court. The court clerk was calling the next docket number on the list when Rena saw Ricky being ushered into the court wearing an orange jumpsuit and shackles. She hoped that he would look around the court and notice her but he only held his head high enough to see what was directly in front of him and making eye contact with the judge as the charges were read aloud.

"Ricky Sheldon is being held for possession of narcotics with intent to sell and tax evasion." The court clerk stepped aside and the DA began his argument against Ricky's release.

"Your honor after months of investigation and surveillance the police uncovered a drug conspiracy involving Ricky Sheldon and a known drug kingpin from New York City with a drug ring covering three states. Two hundred thousand dollars was found on the premises and we have witnesses willing to testify that they have been involved in drug transactions with the defendant. We are suggesting that the defendant be held without bail your honor." The assistant DA stepped back and waited for the defense attorney to make his plea.

"Good morning your honor. My client is pleading not guilty. Mr. Sheldon shares an apartment with his girlfriend and knew nothing about the money found at the premises. We also believe that these witness who have claimed to have dealings with the defendant are making claims with the DA office in a plea deal in exchange that all charges brought against them would be dropped in other cases not related to this. We are asking bail until a hearing date can be set."

Rena held back her tears as they silently fell down her face. Chandelle warned her that Ricky might try to blame her for anything uncovered by the police. But the shock was still overwhelming but she knew she had to compose herself and talk to Ricky as soon as possible. She was thankful that drugs weren't found on the premises but knew that if a jury believed his allegations she could still face prison time.

"Mr. Sheldon you're an example of the dirt and filth that needs cleaned up in the city. However, because there isn't any definite proof that the money found in the premises solely belongs to you and the witnesses against you aren't here in court, bail is being set for fifty thousand dollars. However, there is enough

evidence here to try you in a court of law. Trial is set for thirty days from today." Ricky's body seemed to relax; relieved that he made bail and freedom was now a very real possibility. The court officer grabbed Ricky by the arm to lead him out of the courtroom for transportation back to jail until his bail had been met.

Before walking through the door, Ricky turned to search the courtroom and made eye contact with Rena, giving her a nod of acknowledgement letting her know he was glad she was there for him. Rena left the courtroom in search of the court clerk's office for information concerning bail and visitation.

"Excuse me miss can you help me please" Rena asked the woman at the front desk.

"My boyfriend was just arraigned in Courtroom Two and the judge issued a fifty thousand dollar bond. Can you give me information on obtaining a bondsman and information about when and where I would be able to visit him?" The woman asked his name and when he was arrested and looked in searched her computer.

"Well, his paper work hasn't arrived yet, but if the judge issued a fifty thousand dollar bond, it will take five thousand or ten percent to have him released. The soonest he would be released is possibly this evening or early tomorrow morning depending upon how fast we receive and can process him. You can keep calling our office to check on his release. Anyone here can access that information for you. There is a list of bondsmen listed on the bulletin board directly outside the office. As far as visitation, if he has you on his visitors list you should be able to see him in an hour or two once he gets back to the jail. You can sign in up the street at the jail for a visit." The clerk stated.

"Thank you. You've been very helpful." Rena walked out the office took down a couple of numbers of bondsmen then proceeded up the street towards the county jail.

Game For Fame

Chandelle stood in line at the Electronics Depot waiting at the customer service counter to have her program put on her player's card. She was nervous because she knew what she was about to do could have her thrown behind bars before she even had a chance to try out her plan. She'd spent hours the night before removing traces that the card was connected to the casino by scraping off its logo from the front of the card. She didn't trust putting her program on a blank card because it wasn't certain that the casino machines would recognize her as a platinum cardholder. Besides it was easier to take their card to the cashier and have her load the money on the card without any questions. The success of the plan depended upon her being as discreet and inconspicuous as possible. After the customer before her in line was serviced she stepped to the counter.

"Can I help you?" The young woman asked.

"Yes. I have written a program and I would like it put on the magnetic strip on the back of this card." The clerk took the program from her and placed in the computer drive in front of her.

"What type of program is this? I never recognized anything that looks like this before." Chandelle looked at the young woman trying to figure out a quick lie to divert her interests from her program and asking so many questions.

"It's something that I wrote that I hope will get me a promotion on my job. I hope it makes me a millionaire one day." Chandelle smiled to herself knowing that her last statement was the truth.

"My information is confidential isn't it? I'd hate for someone to try to steal my idea not that I'm accusing you or anything, I'm just trying to get this patented before anybody can come up with a similar idea."

"Oh yeah, our company policy guarantees confidentiality. You'd be surprised how many people use this service for that very reason. In fact, we have the papers to begin the copyright and patent process right here at the customer service counter if you'd like to pay the fee and use our notary service." The clerk stated.

"That's good to know. I'll have to look into it later though. I have a partner and she needs to be involved and she's not here. But I'll be sure to let her know." Chandelle said.

"Are you sure you want me to put it on the strip on the back of this card? It seems to have taken a beaten. We sell cards too if you'd like a new one." The clerk asked pointing to the colorful cards displayed at the end of the counter.

"It is in bad shape huh?" Chandelle chuckled. "No. It has a sentimental meaning to the both of us. We have tried numerous times to get this thing correct but we have run into a few glitches. Each attempt has been made with this card so we decided to keep trying till we get it right. It's funny 'cause my partner thinks that it's the card that has been bad luck but I laughed and said that there wasn't any such thing. So we said that when we get this right we would present it using this card cause it was where it all started. I guess I'm just as superstitious as she is." The clerk seemed to accept her explanation and proceeded to transfer the contents from the CD onto a fresh magnetic strip to be placed on the back of the card. After about five minutes the clerk handed the card to Chandelle.

'Well, it's all done. I wish you and your friend luck. That will be twenty-nine, ninety-nine plus tax." Chandelle reached into her purse taking two twenties from her wallet and waited for her change.

"Thank you and have a nice day." Chandelle took her bag relieved everything had gone as well as t had and left the store.

Chandelle took her keys out and started the car. Putting the car in reverse she backed out of the parking space. Looking out her rearview mirror, chills ran down her spine as the black Charger came up the aisle. Chandelle raced from the space towards the exit making a right onto the parkway and headed towards home.

101

Game For Fame

I know this bitch isn't still following me. I gotta find my phone and call Derek. I told him to handle this trick. Since he won't then I will. I just gotta get home and get my shit. I'm taking her ass out but I got to do it at home where if something bad goes down I can get away clean without any problems from the police. Might even invite the bitch in, then if I kill this bitch I'll be within my legal rights. Chandelle located the phone and called Derek. *Come on Derek answer the fucking phone. Shit!* The answer machine picked up. *Derek it's me. I just left the store and I'm on my way home. Angela is still following me. What the hell is wrong with this crazy heifer? When I left the store and got in my car she was pulling up behind me. I told you to fix this shit! Get your ass over here now! I'm not playin' Derek! You'd better come get her ass before I hurt her. Oh shit! She's right behind me!* Chandelle switched lanes in an attempt to lose her but glancing in her rear view there was Angela right on her tail. Chandelle sped up and swerved between two cars still hoping to lose the crazed woman following her but no matter what she did there was Angela diligent, persistent, still glued to her tail. Changing lanes Angela now in the flow of traffic was forced to pass. Chandelle in her attempts to lose her pulled over to the shoulder of the road took a deep breath and attempted to gather herself.

As soon as Angela noticed the Honda nowhere in sight she too pulled over recognizing that she had been duped and waited for the silver gray Honda to pass. Chandelle's mind raced and when she tried Derek's cell again to no avail she merged into the rush hour traffic confident that she'd finally lost Angela. But with all the patience of Job, Angela remained on the shoulder patiently awaiting the appearance of Chandelle. Moments later, spotting Chandelle, Angela moved back into traffic once again closely on her heels. This time she was alerted of the woman's presence as Angela rammed her from the back. Chandelle was doing eighty now but knew that Angela's Charger with that big block eight was way too powerful for her tiny four cylinder to outrun. Her speedometer now read one hundred and ten and her house was still a good distance away. Quickly she switched lanes to avoid hitting the car in front of her and Angela followed close from behind. *Bam! Bam!* Swerving and narrowly missing a guardrail Angela moved up alongside her slamming into her from the side, partially tearing off her bumper and headlight. Realizing that Chandelle's car was no match for her car, she accelerated and went for the kill. Angela turned her steering wheel to the right to ram Chandelle once more but before she could make impact Chandelle slammed on her brakes. Angela lost control and instead of hitting Chandelle's car she ran onto the shoulder of the highway missing the guardrail completely and tumbled down the hillside.

Shaken, Chandelle pulled over to the side of the highway and got out of the car. Before she made it towards the rail a loud explosion could be heard and a cloud of smoke hovered above the blaze. *I hope that bitch is dead. I told her she didn't know who she was fucking with.* Chandelle assessed the damage of her vehicle and was just glad that she would be able to drive her car home. She heard the police sirens and saw two ambulances approach the scene of the wreck. Chandelle watched as witnesses pointed to the car below and then pointed in her direction singling her out to the officers. Two officers got back in their cars and pulled onto the shoulder stopping next to her vehicle.

"Good afternoon ma'm. Can you tell us what happened here?" The officer took his pad and pencil from his pocket ready to get her side of the story. There was a woman driving the Charger that went off the road, She's my boyfriend's ex. Her name is Angela Washington. She followed me from the mall and was trying to run me off the road. Nothing more than a woman scorned." Chandelle said coolly to the officer.

"Excuse me ma'm," the officer said surprised by her cool demeanor. "Would you please start from the beginning? First tell us your name and explain to me why she was following you." Chandelle watched as two more cruisers pulled up and three or more police cars pulled up near the wreckage followed by news vehicles and ambulances.

"As I told you previously, Mrs. Washington was the wife of my boyfriend. They are going through a divorce and she wanted me to stay away from her husband and was trying her best to ruin my career. Anyway, she has been following me around and today she followed me to the mall and decided to chase me down the highway. I guess her

103

intention was to scare me and 'cause me as much pain and heartache as she could, I honestly don't know what the hell is wrong with her officer." Chandelle motioned to her vehicle.

"Look at my car. She kept running into my car ramming into me until I slammed on my brakes preventing her from hitting me and she lost control and went off the highway." The officer tucked his pen and pad in his breast pocket and went to compare notes with the other officers who pulled up to the scene and was interviewing other witnesses at the scene. The local news station vehicles soon followed but were kept at bay by the yellow tape placed at the scene of the interview.

"Ma'm can I see your license and registration? We're going to need to have a way to get in contact with you later. Your story seems to coincide with the witnesses but we're going to need to investigate the rest of your story. Will you need some medical attention? Are you hurt?" Chandelle shook her head no.

"Are you able to drive your car home?" She said yes and the officer returned her information and walked her to her car. Chandelle drove away before the news reporters pulled up and asked any questions.

Rena gave her drivers license to the intake officer through the window. She sat down and waited until the visitors were called for his floor. *I hope this shit doesn't take long. I can't stand being here with these loud ghetto women talking about shit that's nobody's business and kids running around all over the place unsupervised. I should've listened to my girls a long time ago. I shouldn't even be in this predicament in the first place.* Twenty minutes later the officer called her floor. Rena got in line waiting for her turn to be wanned and frisked before heading to the elevators. Rena walked down the row peeking into each cubicle until she saw Ricky sitting waiting for her visit. Rena saw Ricky through the plastic window and sat down picking up the phone.

"Hey baby. Are you okay?" Rena asked.

Y'vet

"I'm cool but I gotta get out of here. There are some things I need taken care of but I want you to answer something for me first and I need you to tell me the truth." Ricky looked Rena in the eyes 'cause he knew when she was lying. She had a habit of lying when he gave her access to his stash. Every now and then Ricky would leave money in a drawer for her to take out a few hundred so that she could shop or pay some of the bills around the house. She always had some excuse why she needed to spend more than she was supposed to. Her left eye would twitch uncontrollably giving her away every time.

"Did you have anything to do with the police runnin' up in the crib?" Ricky watched her and waited for her to answer.

"No Ricky I didn't. It wouldn't make any sense for me to tell the police that you had anything up in the house. I would've been putting myself in jeopardy and I'm not trying to go to jail. Plus, I didn't know you had anything like that in the house in the first place." Ricky knew she was telling the truth but had to ask her anyway. He knew his boy Tre set him up. He'd deal with him when he got back on the street.

"Ok Rena listen, I'm sorry about what you heard in the courtroom today. That cracker lawyer told me that was my best shot at getting bail. He's just a public defender and I'm going to need you to get in touch with my lawyer to see about these charges." Ricky noticed that Rena became uneasy at the mention of the possibility that the money mentioned in court was suggested as being hers.

"Ricky, I can't go to jail. Please tell me that you aren't going to pin this on me. You know I just lost my job and the little bit of money I'll get from unemployment I'll need to pay the rent and my insurance so my mom can get her treatments." She pleaded.

"I got you Rena. I'm not going to let anyone hurt you as long as..." Ricky didn't finish his sentence instead cocked his head to the side and stroked his chin as if he were up to something.

"As long as what Ricky? Tell me." Rena said concerned.

"As long as you help me get my money back. The police took just about everything I had. That money was going to help me come up and now I've got to start all over. I figured I looked out for you now it's time for you to pay me back." Rena's mouth hung open in shock.

"What do you mean help you get your money back? The police took your money and they aren't giving it back to you Ricky. How am I supposed to get you your money?" Ricky leaned close to the window and said.

'I'm putting you to work for me. I can't trust anybody right now until I find out who snitched and until that's taken care of and you're the only person I can trust. Now if you're not willing to go along with this, I can tell the police about how you were selling drugs and I was just your cover to keep the heat away from you and the money they found belonged to you." Tears began to roll down Rena's face.

"Ricky don't do this. I gave you what you wanted from this relationship. I'm not a drug dealer and I don't want any parts of it. The police will never believe you." Ricky smiled at seeing Rena getting nervous and knew he had her where he wanted her.

"Oh, but they will cause I'm not going down alone. Plus you're just as guilty cause you allowed me to hide the money in your house. If they don't believe that it's yours, you'll do time for being an accessory to the crime or maybe they can charge you for harboring a criminal. You weren't worried when you out spending the loot. Either way you're doing time baby."

"Ricky what if I told you I could come up with a way for you to get your money back? Would you leave my alone and handle the police without getting me involved?" Ricky's smile faded from his face anxious to hear what Rena had to say. Suddenly he became concerned that he was wrong in thinking she didn't have any involvement in his arrest.

"What do you mean get my money back?"

"Well, not the money you lost to the police but I can get it replaced. I don't know how much you lost but I'm sure I can cover your loss." Rena said not looking Ricky in the eye and ashamed that she was about to sell her best friend out to the backstabbing lowlife in front of her.

"And how do you plan on doing that? Your pussy is good but I don't think you can sell fifty thousand dollars worth in the time that I need it." Rena became upset at the thought that he would believe that she would sell her ass like some common trick on the street.

"Fuck you Ricky! I don't plan on selling my body. Chandelle has a plan that would help us make some money. The girls were at her house last weekend and we were talking about how we needed money because we are all in a jam right now. Anyway, she said that she has a way that we can get paid and not worry about money anymore." Ricky sat up in his seat prodding Rena for more information.

"Oh yeah? I know she works for some accounting company or some shit like that. What she going to do? Rip off one of the clients or something?"

"No. It has nothing to do with her job really. I don't have all the details and I don't think we are in a good place to be talking about this right now anyway. What do I need to do to get you released Ricky?" Rena said trying to change the subject.

"At the top of the closet there is a box that has information about how to get in touch with my lawyer. He has been on retainer and has enough money to bail me out. You don't have to worry about a bail bondsmen. He'll take care of everything. I should be out of here by tomorrow evening. I'd like for him to do something about the charges before I'm released if possible to get the bail amount lowered. I also need him to find out about these dudes the police have in custody that have information on me. When I get released I want you at the house so we can continue this conversation about your girl. I don't have a lot of time to come up with this money Rena. I hope you're not lying to me about this." Ricky stated in a threatening tone.

"We'll talk about it later. I'm not lying to you. Our time is almost up and it's not quite five yet so maybe I'll have enough time to make it to see your lawyer today. I'll go bye the apartment and get your stuff and handle your business then I'll be at Chandelle's. I'll be staying there until you are released. I'm not comfortable staying in the apartment alone."

"You have plenty of time to see him. He's been paid to take care of me so he'll answer your call. Just follow the directions on the letter in the box. I'll call you when I get out." The officer can be heard down the hallway. *Time is up! Say your goodbyes and head towards the elevator!* Ricky got up from his chair and blew Rena a kiss. Rena stared at his back as he walked away. *Chandelle please forgive me for what I did. I know I should've discussed this with you first but I didn't have a choice. He's getting out tomorrow and there's no telling what he'd tell the police. I had to tell him. I'm scared of the possibility of going to jail.* Rena left the cubicle and headed back towards the elevator.

Y'vet

Chapter 15

Nia and Rachel exited their cars when they saw Chandelle pull up to the house.

"Chandelle are you okay? I rushed over when I saw you on the news. Girl, from what I saw, I couldn't believe that you were okay. They just showed a car burning over the guardrail then switched to you standing by your wrecked car." Rachel said helping Chandelle from her car.

"I'm okay I guess. I think I may be in shock. I can't believe that crazy bitch."

"What do you mean? Nia said opening Chandelle's front door so that Rachel can help her inside?

Chandelle walked in and asked Rachel to get her something to drink and began explaining the situation from the beginning.

"That crazy ass wife of Derrick's. The bitch followed me again to the mall and followed me trying to kill me by running me off the road." Chandelle took a drink of water and leaned back on the sofa.

"I didn't get a chance to tell you guys what happened before but she followed me the other day and threatened me about seeing Derrick. I was going to kick her ass up in the store then but she walked out before I could get my hands on her. I called Derrick and told him that he needed to do something with her before I hurt her. I haven't talked to Derrick since then. I tried his cell and left a message but he didn't answer."

"Why didn't you call the police then Chandelle?" Rachel asked sitting down.

"I wasn't pressed by her at the time. I just figured she was crazy and jealous. But she did tell me that she sent those pictures to my boss that's why I didn't go to work today. I figured it would be just a matter of time before I was fired. I just didn't want to get the police involved and have to explain everything to them. I'm embarrassed as it is. Plus with this plan I have in the works I didn't want the attention of an investigation to get in the way. But it seems that there is going to be an investigation anyway considering the dumb bitch is dead. Oh Shit! I just thought of something. If you two seen me on the news I know I was recognized by the people at my job. There definitely isn't any way I'm going back there." Chandelle said.

"Damn Chandelle. What are you going to do now?" Rachel said still not believing what happened.

"I'm going to do the damn thing. This may be karma baby. What went down with Angela was going to happen no matter what. The bitch was going to send those pictures to my boss so I was going to lose my job. I just thought that I would be the reason for not getting there on time. So, I was supposed to have that program from work. The way I see it, I was given a second chance. The only difference now is that instead of waiting until the weekend when the casino is crowed, I'm going to try it out tomorrow. By this weekend I should have the whole Angela thing behind me and I could move on with my life. If you want in, we can get rich by this weekend. My plan is to get the money then I'm outta here. I'm leaving town as soon as possible." Chandelle said.

"So, you think this plan is really going to work Chandelle? I mean I have faith in you but with the investigation with Angela and all I would think you'd want to hold off a week or two." Nia said.

"Hell no! I'm not waiting. For what? It either is going to work or it's not. I'll report to the police station and give them everything they need and then move on. There were enough witnesses on the highway to back up my story. I'm not worried about being blamed for her death." Chandelle picked up the remote control from the table to turn on the news for more information about the accident. After watching a commercial Vince Simms was shown standing out on the highway at the scene of the accident. Chandelle turned up the volume to hear the latest update.

Earlier this afternoon there was car a chase involving two drivers leading to the untimely accident of a car being driven over the road barriers here on highway three seventy-six followed by an explosion. Authorities have not been able to identify the driver of the car and at this time a body has not been recovered. Firefighters have been battling the ensuing blaze, which have not allowed them entry into the vehicle. However, medics and the coroner's office are on standby. Witnesses at the scene confirmed a car chase and the occupant of the vehicle being pursued survived with minor injuries. Police have not released the name of the driver of the other vehicle. Chandelle watched as she was shown standing at her vehicle talking to the police. She was interrupted from the newscast as Rena walked in the house calling her name.

"Chandelle, what the hell happened to your car? Are you okay?" Rena said sitting on the couch next to Chandelle.

"I'm okay. I was involved in an accident today. Angela came after me in a car chase and she tore my car up trying to run me off the road. She went over the barriers on the highway. I think the bitch is dead."

"What? That was you? I heard about it on the news on the radio. They said that they weren't giving out any names at this time. Damn Chandelle! When is all this madness going to end?" Rena said thinking about her own situation as well.

"I'll be okay. I was just telling Nia and Rachel that I'm going to the casino tomorrow for the trial run and if everything goes as planned I'll be ready this weekend to pull you in if that's what you want to do. I'm opening up an off shore account tonight and transferring the funds from my 401k. That way after I get the money from the casino I can have a place to send it undetected by the authorities and then get the hell outta here. So, if you girls are in I'd advise that you find a safe haven for your money. Nia I know you can't just up and leave town right away with daughters and all, but you can't have that money just sitting in your checking account without raising some red flags. You don't want that kind of heat on you. Rena and Rachel I advise you come up with a way to hide your money too. You have a couple of days to get ready. Rena what is going on with your situation? Did you go see Ricky? What did he say?" Chandelle said.

"I did have the chance to see him. The police recovered fifty-thousand dollars in my house." Rena said but was bombarded by questions by Rachel and Nia.

"What do you mean the police found fifty-thousand dollars in your house? I knew it! I told you to get rid of that ass hole! He was going to do nothing but bring you down! Nia shouted upset.

"Rena what is going on? Did Ricky get arrested? What are you going to do?" Rachel asked.

"The police ran up in my house with a warrant and searched my place. They found the fifty-thousand that Ricky had stashed and then he was arrested. I went to his arraignment this morning. They gave him bail and he needs five thousand to get out." Rena said making a long story short.

"Well, I hope you leave his ass in there." Nia stated.

"I can't Nia. Somebody obviously let the police know that the money was there. I believe that was the money he was using to make his big move. Anyway, he gave me instructions on how to get in touch with his lawyer so that he can get out. His lawyer has been on retainer and he has money for Ricky to get released. But even if he didn't I would have to come up with a way to get him out." Rena said lowering her head.

"Let me guess. He's threatening you isn't he?" Chandelle said.

"Yeah he is. He said that if I don't help him recoup his money he's going to tell the police that the money found in the apartment was mine." Tears began to slowly run down Rena's face.

"Oh see, no he didn't! We might as well go all out and become full-fledged fugitives of the law. We need to kill that motherfucker. How is he going to threaten you like that? Fuck him!! You don't owe him shit! We can get you a lawyer and fight his allegations. Or we can do as I suggest and have his ass taken out of here. What do you want to do Rena?" Nia said pumped and ready to make a plan.

"Calm down Nia. You're just upset with the male species period. You're not thinking rationally. Rena don't pay Nia any attention. I think we need to slow everything down. I mean everything. We need a solid plan on how all of us are going to move forward here on out. I believe we all are little overwhelmed right now and we are moving too fast." Rachel said being the voice of reason.

"If this wasn't really happening I would think it was funny. I never thought I would see the day that Nia and Rachel would switch personalities. Nia is usually the reserved one telling Rachel to sit her hot ass down somewhere and wait for some man to come to her while Rachel had the going for anything attitude. Now it's the other way around. One things for certain, you can never say what you won't do until the shoe is on the other foot. But Rachel I respect what you're saying but unfortunately we don't have the time to back out and rethink things. The bottom line is that money will take care of all of our problems. Our plan will be successful as long as we know how to handle it once we get it. Rena, I told you earlier that you need to keep close tabs on Ricky and have a grip on where his head is. Whatever you decide to do is on you but do not tell him how you are going to get him the money if you are going to pay him off. You'll have the money to do it but we can't get greedy and we don't want anyone else in on this cause it will do nothing but cause us problems or get us caught." Chandelle said.

Rena looked away because she knew she had already betrayed her best friends trust. *Maybe I can turn this around since she has moved this heist up. I can get the money to Ricky without him being involved and knowing the details and this whole mess will be over.*

"I called the lawyer and he should be out tomorrow. I'm going to stay here again tonight and then move back to my apartment so that I can keep an eye on him. It shouldn't be hard because he doesn't have any money and this thing will be over by the weekend so I should be okay. I decided that I'm going to play the perfect girlfriend and be as loving and supportive as I can. I have to keep him close in order to know what he's up to. I'm not going to jail behind him and his shit." Rena said hoping to reassure her friends as well as herself that things would work out.

"Well, we're out of here. Chandelle I'm glad you are okay and Rena will be here to look after you. Call if you need anything but I'll be calling tomorrow night anyway to see how things went." The women kissed each other and left.

Derek was seen immediately when he entered the emergency room. The head nurse on duty took him to the back and placed clean gauze on his wound and walked him to examination room number one. The doctor came in and removed the gauze and immediately that he'd been stabbed.

"Afternoon Mr. Washington, my name is Dr. Akbar. I'm deeply concerned by the nature of your wounds. The good news is that whatever caused this wound narrowly missed an artery. You're very lucky. We should have you out of here in a about an hour. From the looks of it though it's going to require a few stitches. However, the rules of the hospital are that when cases such as yours come into the hospital, the doctor has to use his discretion on how such a wound happened. It is clear to me that location and the weapon used imply that this was done intentionally so I will have to have a report completed by the police." Derek didn't want to talk to the doctor or the police about what happened. He knew that Angela had to pay for what she done but he wanted to be the one to take care of his own problems involving his family. If there was anything that he hated was having the police involved in his business. Angela had to be dealt with but he wasn't ready to have her thrown in jail or taken away while their daughter was there to witness it. *Fuck! How the hell am I going to get around talking to the police? I looked at my neck and knew I couldn't take care of this shit on my own. Had I known things were going to be questioned I would've gone to the clinic or something. I just didn't feel like sitting in a crowded waiting room.*

"Dr. Akbar, can you please take care of my wound first before I have to talk to the police. I understand the hospital procedures but I need to gather my thoughts before I speak with them. Can you do that for me please?

"Absolutely Mr. Washington. We'd never allow our patients to be in harms way by leaving a wound open to infection. I'll have the nurse come in and prep you for the procedure." The doctor walked out of the examining room and was overheard speaking with the nurse in the hallway. *Please prep Mr. Washington for stitches and administer an injection of Novocain for pain. I'm going to put in a call to the police department concerning his injury. I'll be back in a minute.* Derek thought again about what he was going to say when the police arrived. He realized that there wasn't any way he was going to avoid talking to the investigators.

Fuck it. I'm going to do what I have to do. Chandelle and my daughter are more important and what I should be really concerned about. If this altercation causes me some embarrassment and Angela goes to jail then that's what's going to happen. I need to go on with my life and getting rid of her crazy ass is first on my list. I won't have to worry about my divorce and jumping through hoops now. The judge will have no choice but to rule in my favor.

"Hello. It's Mr. Washington isn't it? I'm nurse Jenkins and I'm here to clean up the area around your wound and give you a little something for pain until the doctor comes back in. He should be here in a minute right about the same time that the medication takes effect."

"Will the medicine cause me to be incoherent or unable to drive home?" Derek asked concerned that he needed to be aware when he explained what happened.

"You'll be fine. It's just a local anesthesia. It doesn't have a lasting effect that will keep you here long after the procedure. It'll have a numbing effect so you won't feel the needle. It doesn't interfere with your understanding or what is going on around you or your thinking capabilities. You will sit here for observation for about an hour then you will be able to sign yourself out." The nurse pulled the tray close to the bed and began cleaning the wound.

"Do me a favor and lean back Mr. Washington I'm going to give you the injection now. Okay you're going to feel a slight pinch. Derek never felt the needle. All he could think about was Angela. Nurse Jenkins was still chattering away.

'Just sit back and relax until the doctor comes in." The numbing kicked in almost immediately. Before he could fully relax the doctor came into the room to start the procedure.

"Mr. Washington are feeling the effects of the medicine? Do you feel any numbness? Derek nodded. Okay, I'm going to give you another minute or so and then I'm going to get started. However, I called the police department and they stated that they are short officers on duty tonight so you may have to wait awhile for them to arrive. I have already made arrangements for a recovery room to be set up for you to and await their arrival. You will not be charged for the service considering the circumstances." The stitches were done in no time and Derek was placed in a wheel chair and taken up to the third floor and to his room. The nurse's aid helped Derek on the bed and placed two pillows behind his head.

"Are you comfortable Mr. Washington? Want me to adjust the bed for you? Is there anything else I can get you?"

"Do you have a remote for the television?" The gentlemen pointed to the table near the bed. Derek turned on the television to catch the last round of the PGA championship where Tiger was three under par. Just before Tiger was able to tee off on the eighteenth hole the program was interrupted by a breaking news flash. *Damn! Why do they have to interrupt right before the good part? What the hell is it this time?* Derek listened while he waited to see Tiger win another championship.

Reporters are at the scene of a horrible accident on I-376. A car was reportedly seen chasing after another vehicle before being pushed off the barrier and exploding on impact. Derek jumped up in bed when he saw that Chandelle was pulled over on the side of the road next to her car that the reporter said was involved in the altercation.

What the fuck? Why would Chandelle be on the parkway with her car tore up? Who the hell is chasing her? And why? Oh No! Angela tell me you didn't do this! Derek turned up the volume to try to catch the rest of the broadcast.

Firefighters are on the scene but a body has yet to be recovered. Names of the other individuals involved have not yet been released. Updates on this story and more at eleven. Derek jumped out of the bed, the panic obvious. The report left to many unanswered questions. Was Chandelle all right? Where was Angela? Was she involved?

His phone has been turned off since he entered the hospital so he didn't know if Chandelle had been trying to reach him or not. He'd intended to call her once he left the hospital to tell her what had happened when he went to the house to confront her. *Damn! I knew she was mad when she ran out the house after she stabbed me but I thought she was going to go chill out somewhere and get her a drink like she always does. I never thought that she would go after Chandelle. I got to get out of here. I'll talk to the police later. If she's dead like it looks like she is it won't matter anyway. If anything they will be trying to take me down the station to question me about these incidences being connected. I ain't got time for this shit. I gotta get the hell outta here.* Derek grabbed his shoes from the side of the bed and walked to the door looking out that he wouldn't be noticed when he walked down the hall and got on the elevator unnoticed.

Y'vet

Chapter 16

Derek stood outside Chandelle's house ringing her doorbell repeatedly. He knew she was home because there were lights on on the second floor and her car was parked in the driveway. Derek also recognized Rena's car parked out front by the curb. He thought about yelling her name to get her to answer the door but thought against alerting the neighbors and the last thing he needed was for one of them to call the police. Derek banged on the door until he heard the window slide open on the second floor.

"What the hell do you want Derek? I didn't answer the door for a reason. I don't want to be bothered with your ass!" Chandelle said.

"Please come and open the door. I really need to talk to you about what happened today. I need to know that you're okay. Come on baby. I don't want the neighbors all in our business." Derek said as he walked backwards to get a view of her face and plead his case.

"I'm fine. Now get the fuck off my property or I'll call the police." Derek shook his head not believing that Chandelle was being so unreasonable. *I can't believe she is acting like this. Damn! This is the second time today that I'm being threatened with the police. First thing a woman wants to do is bring the police in our business. I love her but I'm starting to think she and no other woman is worth all this damn drama.*

"Chandelle, would you listen to me. I did as you asked and talked to Angela. Just give me a chance and let me try to explain what happened. Listen, I saw the news and I'm concerned. Just come and open the door. Let me see you so at least I know that you're okay. I just need to see for myself and know that that crazy ass bitch didn't harm you in any way. Just open the door baby. I really need to see you. If you don't want to be bothered after that then I'll leave. Okay?"

120

"After you say what you have to say Derek I want you to go and I'm not playing any games with you. You have five minutes." Chandelle slammed the window shut and went down the steps to open the door.

"Come in Derek. Five minutes then I want you out." Chandelle stepped to the side of the entry way and Derek walked into the living room and sat down.

"Chandelle, I want to know how you're doing but I don't think you're in the mood to answer any of my questions. So, let me tell you what happened when I left to speak to Angela. I told her that I wasn't going to allow her to interfere in our lives and I let her know that all the games where over."

"How did you do that Derek? The marriage was over a long time ago let you tell it. What makes your saying something now any different than before? That bitch doesn't care about your threats. Isn't that obvious? When has she ever listened to anything you've said? I've always thought the bitch was crazy and after today I'm convinced. Do you know what that silly ass wife of yours did? No, I'm not even going to get into that right now. I'm still shaken. But you know what Derek? I can't believe that you really and truly believe that you can rationalize this situation with someone who isn't dealing with a full deck of cards. I mean this woman is certifiable. She's crazy Derek. She really is crazy. Something is truly wrong there. She needs to be institutionalized or put down or something. I'm tired and through. I guess you saw the news today. It was Angela chasing me on the parkway. Did you see my car? That bitch wrecked my car Derek! She tried to kill me. I warned you that if you didn't handle her that I would. Well, guess what? The bitch is dead and I'm not a least bit upset about it. The only person I feel sorry for is that little girl of yours because she was being raised by two fucked up parents." Derek looked at Chandelle. The hurt and shock evident in his face.

"That's right both of you are fucked up individuals. You are as bad as her by allowing her to continue to have custody of your child. You knew she was crazy and possessive but your needs came first and you allowed that little girl to stay there to deal with that woman. Now you have to go and explain to her that her mother is dead. You ain't shit and I can't believe that I was in love with you. I don't want you to come past my house and please don't call me. There isn't a chance in hell that we'll ever be together." Chandelle watched as Derek went through a series of mixed emotions that showed on his face. Calming down Chandelle continued,

"If you had been truthful from the beginning maybe things wouldn't have ended this way. Now I have to deal with the police, I lost my job and I'm left trying to figure out how to put my life back together." Derek reached for Chandelle realizing now that he may have lost the best thing that had ever happened to him.

"Baby, I'm sorry. I'm really sorry for everything. I wish there was something that I could do to take it all back or maybe fix things so that we have a fresh start." Chandelle pulled her hand away from Derek not wanting to succumb to his advances like before.

"I'm sorry too Derek. Please lock the door when you leave." Chandelle turned away from Derek fighting back tears she didn't want him to see. The last thing she wanted was for him to take advantage of her moment of weakness. She waited until she heard the door shut behind him as he left. She then turned off the lights and headed for the steps to her room.

Chapter 17

Ricky caught a cab to the apartment he and Rena shared. He thought about calling Rena to pick him up so she could continue explaining how she and her girl were going to rob the casino but changed his mind. Ricky wanted an opportunity to look through the house and check the floorboards in the bedroom to make sure his package was still there. *Damn I'm glad that I put that lawyer on retainer. As soon as I started hearing that shit on the street about Tre and my money started caming up missing I knew I couldn't trust nobody when it came to takin' care of my business. Baby girl never gave me a reason not to show her love and I knew she wouldn't hurt me as long as I kept the money flowin' but she started not to have any control over what she spent. She was out here flossin' and spending my money like the shit grew on trees. I knew that if something was to go down I couldn't depend on her to get my ass out of jail if I needed her to. I'm going to get my shit and package it up and collect the dough that's owed to me. Rena gonna make good on what I lost. Fuck that! It ain't comin' out her pocket so she ain't losing nothin' anyway. Bitch owes me. She gonna kick me some cash from what she and her girl got planned then I'm getting the fuck outta town. But first I'm going to handle Tre, take care of this bullshit the five-o tryna give me time for, collect my money from Rena, and then I'm gone.* Ricky made it to the apartment and opened the door realizing the apartment was in the same condition it was in when he got picked up. *Damn! Rena wasn't lyin when she said she broke camp. They fucked this place up. She needs to bring her ass on home and come clean this shit up. A nigga needs a shower, a good meal and some trim.* Taking two stairs at a time he ran towards the bedroom pulling back the carpet where he hid his stash. Pulling up the floorboards next, Ricky pulled out the small, metal safe and turned the combination lock. After seeing the money still safe and sound he lowered the box in the hole once again before back on top and placed the rug back into its proper place. Ricky pulled out his cell phone and called Rena.

"Hey baby it's me. Where are you?" He asked after she picked up on the first ring.

"Hi honey! Are you out? Where are you? "

"I been out for a minute now."

Oh, baby that's great! I was surprised when I saw your phone number show up on my phone. I didn't think you were getting out today. What time did you get out?"

" I was released this morning but I had to talk to my lawyer for a minute then I just decided to catch a cab and come back to the crib. How long before you get here?"

So why are you calling so late?

"Like I said I had some business to take care of. Where are you?"

" I'm at Chandelle's. Where are you? I'll come get you now."

"I'm straight just hurry up and get home. I still need to go out and take care of a couple of things. I'll see you in a few."

"Give me a minute and I'll be right there. I know you're hungry so I'll pick up something on the way home. What do you have a taste for?"

"Whatever you pick up is fine."

"Okay, baby. Just relax if you can. I know the place is a mess but I'll make it up to you when I get there baby."

Ricky hung up the phone not allowing Rena to answer. *Yeah if things go like I planned, I'm out of here by next week.*

Rena left the kitchen and walked to the living room to talk to Chandelle about her plans on going back to her apartment but she wanted to be sure that her girl could handle being alone right through here. Rena had overheard the conversation between Chandelle and Derek last night when they were talking in the living room. She wanted to confront her then but knew it was best to give Chandelle her space. Now that she was leaving he needed to know what her friend was thinking especially since tonight was the night she was going to the casino. It was important that Chandelle had a clear head and didn't make any mistakes because she had Derek on her mind and in her heart.

"Hey girl, I just got off the phone with Ricky. He's at the apartment."

"Oh Yeah? How did he sound? Are you going to be okay?" Chandelle asked looking up from the book she was reading.

"I guess he's okay. I'm sure we have a lot to talk about but it's you that I'm more concerned about right now. How are you feeling? I know Derek was here last night and you had time to think about everything that went on yesterday."

"I'm fine. I had plans on going by the police station today to complete a formal report about the accident yesterday and get updated on any information the police may have uncovered. I want to go to them rather than have them come looking for me. It's also going to free me up to go to the casino tonight. I don't need any interruptions tonight."

Rena studied Chandelle's body language to get a real feel on how she was feeling. Rena knew Chandelle long enough to know when she was lying or worse trying to fool herself.

"What about Derek Chandelle?"

"What about him Rena?" Chandelle said looking back into her book attempting to read where she left off.

125

"I overheard the two of you last night Chandelle. I know damn well you didn't just get over that man overnight. You love him. Are you sure you can handle going through with this right now?"

"Look Rena. You don't have to worry about me concerning some man. Yeah, I loved him—past tense—but it didn't work out. What am I supposed to do sit around and cry over it? You know I ain't never sweat no man and I'm not going to start now. Now let's concentrate on the future and leave our past mistakes alone. You wit' me? We have business to take care of. Neither of us has any money that will last us longer than a couple of months but we have an opportunity to not have to worry about money for a long time if not for life. Go handle you business and call me tomorrow and I'll fill you in on what happens tonight. Okay? Don't worry about me." Chandelle put her book on the table and stood up to give her best friend a hug.

"Now go and check on Ricky. I love you girl. Thanks for being concerned." Rena pulled her purse strap up on her shoulder not wanting to make eye contact feeling guilty because of her betrayal against the woman she considered a sister more than a friend.

"Okay. I'll call you tomorrow. Stay safe." Rena walked to the door locking it behind her.

Chapter 18

After an hour of waiting at the rental car agency for approval from the insurance company for a car Chandelle left smiling in a brand new Cadillac Escalade. She felt strong and powerful driving such a huge vehicle. She felt like she couldn't be touched by anything or anyone. She always wanted to own such an elegant car and never test-drove anything on that level because she knew she could never afford such an extravagance. *I wish I were driving something like this when that crazy bitch Angela came after me. I woulda ran over her ass and she wouldn't have had a chance to chase me down. She'd been dead first. Damn this truck is nice. I'm going to have to go out and buy myself some like this. Maybe I'll go Mercedes or Jaguar. Shit, if this shit works out the way I planned it I'll have everything that I've ever wanted. The hell with being broke.* Chandelle was already in a much better mood despite heading to the police department to be interrogated about her personal life, which she believed, wasn't anybody's business but her own. *If I gotta tell them about my affair with Derek and the pictures then so be it. I really don't give a damn right now. From now on I have a new attitude and it's not going to be about anything but Chandelle. It's time to do me. I'm going to look out for my girls then I'm leaving town to make a new life somewhere else. I don't care or have time to worry about any shame or embarrassment.* Chandelle pulled into the police station and asked the desk clerk to speak to the officer in charge. She gave her name and explained why she was there and stated that she wanted to give a full deposition. The desk clerk pointed to the small crowd of people waiting and informed her that she could join them and have a seat in the waiting area and someone would be with her shortly. Five minutes later she heard her name.

"Ms. Carter?" Chandelle rose from the bench in the waiting area when she heard her name.

"Hi. My name is Officer Gaines. Would you follow me please? I'll be asking you some questions this afternoon concerning the accident yesterday. Please have a seat in the room. Would you like something to drink before we get started?" Chandelle smiled to herself thinking that if the circumstances were different she would love to have a sip of some of Officer Gaines. He was tall dark and handsome just like Chandelle liked them but she quickly recovered from her thoughts concentrating on why she was there in the first place.

"Yes. I'd like a glass of water please." The officer pulled back the chair and waited for Chandelle to take her seat standing behind her staring at her from head to toe a lot longer than necessary. Returning with her drink he grabbed his pen and pad and explained to her what would be expected during the interview and reminded her that she was permitted to have council available. He explained that there was already an investigation in motion and she wasn't being charged at this time for any crime. After Chandelle stated that she had nothing to hide and didn't feel a need for council, Officer Gaines turned on the recorder and began the interview. Chandelle stated her full name and address and proceeded to answer the officers' questions.

"Ms Carter what was your relationship to Ms. Washington?

"I didn't really know Ms. Washington until a few weeks ago. I have been having an affair with Derek Washington for the last two weeks. I didn't know until recently that Derek was married. Mr. Washington has been going through a messy divorce. He didn't have a choice but to tell me that he was married. We had plans on marrying later this year."

"How did you find out that she knew about the affair between you and Mr. Washington?

"Ms. Washington sent an envelope to my home containing some pictures of a sexual nature of myself and Derek in bed along with pictures of Derek and a woman I was not familiar with and pictures of he and his wife. She also sent a note stating that she sent the pictures to my boss in an attempt to ruin my reputation and make me lose my job."

"Would you still have possession of those pictures and the note stating her intentions Ms Carter?"

"Yes. I think so. I know I didn't throw them away. They are in my house somewhere. Why do you want them?"

"Well, the pictures and the letter would support your story on her motive for chasing you on the highway. I'd like you to bring that information to the station as soon as possible. It would help in solving and closing this case as soon as possible, which I'm sure you're anxious to do." Officer Gaines looked deeply into Chandelle's eyes and offered a warm smile.

"I'd like to also inform you that after the wreckage was cleared there was no body found. Investigators are still continuing to determine what that means. It is probable that the body was burned beyond recognition but when a body is not found the case remains open. Well, Ms. Carter I believe that will be all for right now unless you have any questions." Chandelle shook her head no.

"Okay. Well if you can stay here for another ten minutes or so, your deposition will be translated onto paper and you will need to read it and sign it. You will then be free to go. If there are any further questions someone will contact you." Handing her his card Officer Gaines excused himself and left the room.

Rena pulled up to her apartment complex and was surprised to see the large garbage bags outside of her apartment door. Opening the apartment door Rena was shocked to see that Ricky had begun cleaning up. She placed her purse and keys on the coffee table and walked to the kitchen to grab plates for the take-out Chinese she promised to bring home for them to share.

"Ricky! I'm home honey! Give me a minute to grab us some food and I'll bring it up to the bedroom in a minute!" Rena placed the food in the microwave and pulled out a serving tray from the kitchen pantry and begun preparing their food. She headed up the stairs to find Ricky lying across the bed lightly snoring. She placed the tray down and stared at him acknowledging how fine he was and that he would make a hell of a husband if his work ethics and energy were directed in another direction. *Damn he's fine. Why couldn't he do the right thing and get a job like everybody else? Oh well, I just need to clear my head and make the best of a bad situation. One more week and everything will be fine. I got to keep telling myself just one more week.* Rena walked towards the bed and planted a kiss on his forehead awakening Ricky from his sleep.

"Hey sleepy head, are you hungry?" Rena said and smiled.

"Yeah, hungry for you." Ricky reached for Rena's waist and pulled her on the bed on top of him.

"I need you baby. Take your clothes off and get in bed with me. We can eat later." Ricky pulled Rena's shirt over her head and tossed it to the end of the bed then quickly tugged her jeans down from her hips and threw them to the floor.

"Damn Ricky slow down! It's not going anywhere!" Rena said while she pulled off her underwear making herself comfortable. Ricky snatched back the sheet Rena held to cover her and spread her legs wide open pulling out his nine inches without shedding his boxers and mounted her like a dog in heat.

"Ow Ricky! It hurts! Slow down!" Rena said trying to get some control over his aggressiveness by bucking her hips to slow him down. Ricky grabbed her arms and pinned them over her head and thrusted harder causing her head to bang into the headboard keeping her still so that he could have leverage in pushing his dick in as far as it would go. Rena held back any attempts to stop him and closed her eyes hoping that he would soon finish. Finally, she heard loud grunts and moans and felt the cum oozing from between her legs. Drenched in sweat, Ricky rolled over on his back breathing heavily regaining his composure.

"What the fuck was that Ricky? Huh? You hurt me! So you're into raping me now?" Rena said attempting to wrap the sheet around her and leave for the bathroom to clean up. Ricky grabbed her arm not allowing her to move.

"Lay down Rena. Ain't nobody rape your ass. You know a nigga was down for a couple of days. I just needed to get that one off that's all. Damn! Chill out! I'll take care of you later." Ricky stuck his dick back into his boxers and got up to get the tray and brought it over to the bed.

"This looks good. Here. Let me fix you a plate." Ricky placed the food in front of Rena and grabbed a teriyaki wing from his plate and laid down on the bed next to her. Rena rolled her eyes and picked up the fork and nibbled on the food in front of her.

"You were down a couple of days in the county Ricky not years in the penitentiary." Ricky ignored her and said,

"So did you have a chance to talk to your girl?"

"What do you mean talk to my girl Ricky?

"About what happened. Did you talk to her?"

"If you're asking if I told her about the police coming into the house and taking you to jail, yes I told her. But I already told you that."

"I know you did. She had to know why you stayed at her crib for the last few days. I'm talking about the money and the fact that you need to come up with the loot that was taken by the cops."

131

"Ricky, I know you're not blaming me for the cops running up in this house. I live here too. I still don't understand why you are forcing me to replace what you lost."

"I didn't say you brought the cops up in here. But what I am saying is that I took care of your ass for the last year so now it's time to pay me back."

"Ricky, I was your woman. You did as any man would do in a relationship. I don't owe you anything."

"Well, if you feel that way then you won't mind doing half the time I'm looking at for havin the cash in here in the first place. You knew what type of nigga I was and what I was doin. Don't get stupid now that the shit ain't good no more. You wanna talk all that equality shit. I coulda got pussy anywhere. So, if I was your man then you willin' to walk off half this time. Rena put down her fork and wiped the tears beginning to run down her face. Ricky turned and looked in her eyes and said,

"Look baby, I ain't tryna hurt you. I love you to death. I probably wouldn't have even asked until you said something about your girl takin out that casino. I figured it wasn't costing you shit. She's the one doin it and because you and her are fam I knew she was gonna look out." Ricky lied. He knew he would put her ass out their on the block if he needed to, to get some of his cash back. Rena believed that Ricky loved her and things would have been different if the circumstances weren't what they were.

"I believe you Ricky. I just wish that things were different that's all. I don't want to see anything bad happen to you." Ricky smiled to himself knowing that he had her in the palm of his hands.

"I did mention to Chandelle that you needed some money. She was supportive and told me that what I did with my share was on me. However, she did make it clear that I was to keep the details of what she was going to do to myself. I didn't tell her that I told you. Ricky you can't let her find out that you know." Rena said with pleading eyes.

132

"Baby you know I wouldn't say anything to her. We don't talk or see each other like that anyway. It's been over a month since she been to the crib. Didn't you say that everything was going down in the next couple of days?" Ricky asked prodding the plan from her.

"Yeah, in fact she moved it up. While you were away Chandelle got caught up in some mess involving Derek's soon to be ex-wife. To make a long story short, his ex followed Chandelle in a car chase and she ended up going over the guardrail and her car went up in flames."

'Get the fuck outta here! Damn! That's some fucked up shit! Is Chandelle okay?"

"Yeah she's okay, better than I would have expected. You figured she lost her man and is part of an investigation all at the same time. Plus she lost her job cause the bitch did some scandalous shit by sending some photos to her boss." Rena leaned over the tray and sipped the soda from her glass she brought to the room earlier.

"Wow! That's the type of bitch a nigga likes to have on his team." Ricky shielded his head from the slap that Rena gave him across the back of his head.

"Watch your mouth Ricky. That's my sister girl you're talking about." Ricky started laughing.

"I was just saying baby. When you're in the business I'm in a nigga likes having a ride or die chick by his side. She took that shit and now she's about to rob a casino? That's some real gangsta shit!"

"Whatever Ricky. Anyway, she's going to test out things at the casino tonight. If things go as she plans it's on for tomorrow night." Ricky's attention rose when he heard that tidbit of information.

"Tonight huh? She's going over there tonight?" Ricky asked scheming to himself.

"Yeah, that's the plan. She went past the police station today to handle some business so the police won't come looking for her to answer questions and get them out the way."

"Smart woman. Now come here and let's finish what we started. I don't have long baby. I need to go out here and see what's going on in the streets" Ricky grabbed Rena's face and kissed her passionately on the lips before pushing her back onto the mattress.

Chapter 19

Chandelle stood in line at the cashier window waiting to deposit the five hundred dollars she withdrew from the ATM machine onto her players' card. Anxious but cautious she scanned the room behind her trying to find the least conspicuous place where she would draw the least attention. Chandelle wanted to get her money fast and get out safely. She thought about going to the dollar machines but her aim tonight was to find out if her scheme was going to work properly. She decided that she would find five-dollar slot machines surrounded by a few players so she could blend in but wanted no parts of the high rollers room because it tended to draw too many curious onlookers wishing they had the money to risk twenty to fifty dollars a spin.

"Can I help you?" the cashier asked.

"Yes. Can you deposit five hundred to my players' card please? Chandelle said passing over the money and her card. The cashier took her money and smiled counting out the money in hundred dollar stacks in clear view of the cameras above. The cashier then typed in her account number from the front of her card and passed it back to Chandelle. *Thank God I got passed that hurdle. She didn't notice that the card had been tampered with. I wish she would hurry the hell up.*

"Okay Ms. Carter. You're ready to go. Here is your pin number that you will need to put in the machine. You have also earned points towards the buffet and bar. Good luck and thank you for coming to the River's Edge." Chandelle gathered her card and slip and headed towards the five-dollar slots. Five machines were available while three were filled with two women playing two machines at the same time. Chandelle was in awe that these women were feeding twenty dollars simultaneously in two machines one on each side of them. *Damn! How the hell can these old biddies afford to gamble like this? It doesn't make any sense to work your entire life to turn around and spend your pension money in a damn machine. I mean I love to gamble and I thought I might have needed some gamblers anonymous meetings but I wasn't spending more than a dollar a spin and gambling maybe once a month. That shit they're doing is crazy.*

"Excuse me. Anybody playing this machine?" Chandelle asked the woman engrossed in her two machines. She had a bag and coat hanging over the chair in front of the machine Chandelle wanted to play.

"Oh no sweetheart, you can play here. I was saving this machine for my girlfriend but she decided to give up on it. She already lost a shit load of money in it. So, it's either going to pay off big for you or take you dry. I just left my things there because I didn't want to put them on the floor. I'm superstitious you know. Put your purse on the floor and you'll never have any money." The woman continued to babble on but Chandelle just waited patiently for her to remove her things. She didn't have any interest in making any new friends but smiled as if she heard every word.

"Thank you." Chandelle sat down and put her card in the machine and waited for the prompt to appear in the window.

Welcome to The River's Edge Chandelle Carter. You have twenty dollars in casino cash and a cash deposit balance of five hundred dollars. Chandelle entered her pin and hit the button indicating she wanted to spend the casino bonus cash first. *Press the amount you wish to spend.* Chandelle programmed the machine to reflect that she had fifty thousand dollars in casino cash to gamble. She knew there was little risk in the amount. The casino took in millions of dollars a quarter and this trip was just a trial run. She only needed to gamble long enough to see if her balance stayed the same mirroring the *Accounting Pro* program. If it stayed the same she knew she was home free. At the end of the night she would just need to transfer the players' bonus money to her cash balance at the cashier window then transfer the money to her checking account when she got home. The trick was turning the players' money to real cash. She needed to bet fifty thousand dollars worth of casino cash so that it would transfer to her cash balance. *I could be here all night trying to spend this bonus money. I can't believe that this is the one time that I don't want to hit a*

136

jackpot. That would cause bells to go off and I would have to answer to the IRS. I hope I go through this casino cash quick. Chandelle pressed the maximum bet spending twenty dollars on her first spin. She watched as a bell, diamond and cherry appeared in the three wheel windows. *Yes! Nothing! Okay so I spent twenty dollars, let me check my cash balance to see if my cash balance increased going from five hundred to five hundred twenty.* Chandelle pressed the account balance button and sure enough her balance registered five hundred and twenty dollars. *Forty-nine thousand nine hundred and eighty more dollars to go* she said to herself. Chandelle called over the waitress and ordered a diet soda and resumed hitting the maximum bet button.

Chapter 20

Ricky hit Main street around ten o'clock waiting for his boys to hit the block. He didn't call anybody to announce that he was released from jail because he wanted to check out if business was being done as usual. He'd know right away if his boy's were loyal or taking orders from somewhere else. Besides, his plan was to sit in the cut and watch out for Tre. He figured that the crew knew he was caught up because the plan was for him to meet them at the safe house on Saturday to collect his cash and give his boys their packages for the weekend. When he didn't show, protocol was to make the rounds in the streets for a possible hit then check the roster at the jail. He knew word was out that he got picked up. Ricky only had to wait an hour before Tre pulled up calling Mouse over to his car. Mouse worked the corner off Main for the past three years. Ricky liked Mouse and respected his game. Mouse never came up short on money and took care of his mother and little sister. If Mouse had a beef with somebody or felt his feet were being stepped on he always manned up and went straight to the source. Nobody fucked with Mouse and Mouse didn't fuck with nobody. Tre rolled down the window to his Lexus and passed a package through the window. Mouse looked in the brown bag and passed what looked like a roll of money to Tre. Ricky knew right away that something was up and Tre was moving in. Business was never conducted in the streets out in the open. He prided himself on keeping his workers low key and undercover. None of his boys were picked up since he took over the streets. There was no need to be careless. *I told these mutha fuckas that if they run out of product or heavy on money they are to come off the street and wait till they were called to the house to re-up. Fuck that! Ain't nobody hungry out here! Tre always gotta floss and remind niggas that he's the man. His ass is gonna go down for being stupid.* Ricky waited till the transaction was completed then he slowly moved behind Tre to follow him as he pulled away from the curb. Ricky followed Tre for about two miles before Tre pulled into the driveway of a brick ranch located on the East Side. Ricky parked down the street remaining unnoticed to watch his next move. Ricky knew Tre was running his own game because he was dirty from the transaction he made with Mouse and he wouldn't be out on a social call ridin with cash and drugs. Ricky needed to know who Tre was working with and wondered why he was makin moves in enemy territory. *This nigga is gonna get fixed. I just gotta figure out how and when. I ain't even gonna ask any questions cause right now I don't give a fuck. I just need to know what kind of players he's bringing into the game. I don't want to bring down any heat on the block. Tre has been my boy but he betrayed me, and he never came to see about a nigga when he was down. He stole my shit and left me for dead with the cops. I'm gonna let them niggas fight for what's left.*

Ricky watched Tre get out of his car and take out the package he received from Mouse and place it in his backpack. Tre walked to the house and knocked. The curtains opened slightly then closed. Seconds later the front door opened and a thug dressed in a Celtics throwback layered over a white tee with a pair of jeans and fresh white Forces hugged Tre and ushered him in. Ricky immediately recognized Carlos as a small time New York dealer. He'd wanted to do business a few months ago but Ricky had turned him down because he wasn't willing to cut him any deals worth his money. Besides, Ricky didn't like his style. He had a loud mouth and he was always sportin' something with the Celtics logo on it. It made him stand out and Ricky knew right away he was trying to get a rep and make a name for himself. He wondered how Tre was able to hook up with him behind his back. Tre traveled to New York for the meeting but Ricky didn't take him along to talk business. Tre was handy with his glock and Ricky felt safe with his boy close behind him but Tre didn't have any business sense and was too eager to make it big without putting in the work to find the best dope for the money.

Tre entered the house and closed the door behind him. The lights in the front of the house went off but the lights came on in a room towards the back of the house. Ricky decided to go back to his car and wait. *What the fuck this nigga up to? I see the rumors in the streets were true. It was Tre all along skimming money off the top. He spent the last couple of months making examples in the street to cover his shit. Fuck! This nigga caught me slippin'. Well, we goin to see what's up tonight.*

An hour passed when Ricky saw Tre walk out the front door of the house to his car. Tre slung his backpack from around his shoulders and placed it in the backseat of the car. He then got in and pulled off with Ricky following far enough behind him to go unnoticed. Ricky followed Tre to his house and waited until he got out his car and entered his house. Ricky waited ten minutes and decided to get out and ring the doorbell. Ricky heard Tre walking towards the door and watched as he pulled back the curtain from the small window. Tre unlocked the door and opened it greeting Ricky.

"What's up my nigga?" Tre stepped out onto the porch closing the door behind him.

"I got a girl inside. Let's talk out here."

Tre looked at Ricky trying to keep his composure from telling of his surprise at seeing Ricky standing in front of him.

Lying ass nigga. I'll play along for a minute. This muthafucka think I'm stupid. Ricky thought to himself.

"You tell me nigga. I've been down for the last couple of days and you haven't come to see about a nigga. What's up with that man?" Ricky moved closer to Tre causing him to back into the door of the car.

"I heard man. I was comin' to check on you tomorrow. Was out here tryin' to make sure this money we had out here was straight in case I needed it to make bail for you."

"Oh yeah? Tell you what. Give me what you were bailing me out with now." Tre stood still not knowing whether to go for the trunk for what he had left from the deal he just made or play off his man and try to stall him until he was able to come up with his cut of the weekends take.

"Where's my money man? Better yet tell me what you were doing over on the other side of town? I've been following you for the last couple of hours. I got some serious problems with how you been handlin' business out here on the streets Tre. You got five minutes to give me some straight answers or we gonna have some problems out here." Tre thought about lying to Ricky but was tired of living in his shadows and decided to come clean about what he'd been up to.

"I'll have your money by the end of the week. I can give you half of what is owed to you from what we had on the street but I made my own connect and doin' my own thing now. When I get rid of what I have I can give you what's yours. I'm steppin' out man. It's time for me to be my own man and run my own crew."

"So it's like that? You the man now Tre? You been going behind my back stealin' my dough off the top, runnin my crew, and now you the man? Nigga we been boys for years and you goin' to do some foul shit like that? How the police know to run up in my crib the other day when it was by coincidence the day I was meeting with the connect? You know anything about that Tre?" Tre reached back to open the car door he was leaning into to have easy access to his gun under the drivers side seat. He didn't want to take his boy down but knew that he couldn't allow Ricky to get in the way of his plans. If he needed to kill Ricky then so be it.

"You look a little nervous Tre. I'll help you out. Don't even answer that last question cause I know the answer. Don't open the door for your gun. Back away from the car towards me so I won't have to shoot you." Ricky gestured towards his gun under his shirt hidden inside his waistband.

"Man, you know we better than that. I'm not even trying to go out like that. I wouldn't shoot you man." Tre moved towards Ricky away from the car. When he got within reach, Tre pushed Ricky causing him to fall backwards to the ground giving him time to turn to his car and reach for the door. Tre dove inside reaching for his gun when Ricky let off two shots; one landing in the back door window shattering glass onto the sidewalk and the other in the back of Tre's head splattering blood over

141

the front seat of the car. Ricky ran to the car recovering the backpack he saw Tre stash in the trunk and quickly got in his car and sped away.

Chandelle looked down at her watch and noticed it was ten and the cashiers' window closed in an hour. There was close to thirty thousand dollars in her account nowhere close to the fifty thousand she programmed on her card. *This shit ain't gonna work at the pace I'm playing. I would need to come to the casino for two weeks before being able to get enough money to retire on. The only chance I have is to head towards the high rollers room where I can bet the maximum and get more money in less time.* Chandelle stood looking towards the high rollers club and noticed that there were only three men playing and five empty rows available to play the slots. *Well, I've come this far I might as well go for it all. I should be able to clear the other twenty thousand if I play the twenty- dollar machines and have the money transferred by eleven before the cashier windows close.* Chandelle gathered her things retrieved her card from her machine and headed towards the high rollers club. She decided to play two rows from the gentleman playing a ten-dollar triple reel slot machine. *I guess I'll sit here and play. Any of these machines will do. Under any other circumstances I would never be in here in the first place. I don't want to draw attention to myself by being too far away from the players in the room as if I have something to hide. I'm just gonna play this machine and treat it like a job. Whatever I do in an hour will have to do.* Chandelle inserted her card and pushed the lever placing her bet at forty dollars a spin. Her first spin collected her a one hundred and eighty dollar return. *Damn! Three single bars hit like this? I should have been playing in this room from the start!* She smiled to herself excitedly.

"Wow! Nice hit ma'am! A few more of those and you're gonna be leaving out of here owning the place." Chandelle turned around and noticed she was being watched by one of the attendants that worked at the casino.

"Yeah, that was nice huh? I hope my luck keeps up. It sure would be nice to leave here a winner tonight." She said trying to blow off the attendant as if she was already losing a lot of money.

"Well, I wish you luck. Can I get you something to drink?"

"No. Thank you. I'll only be here for a little while then I'm heading out." Chandelle smiled and reached for her bag stalling for time as if she was trying to retrieve something hoping the attendant would keep moving. The attendant wished her a good night and she sighed with relief when he walked away. What she didn't know was that there was someone else watching her. In the corner of the room Ricky was sitting at a five-dollar slot machine wondering how Chandelle was pulling off the heist. *What the fuck is she doing? Anybody can come in and feed the machines and hope to win. I should have got more information on how she was pulling this shit off. I'm watching this bitch and I've already lost two hundred trying to figure out her game. This bitch is going to give me all her loot and repay me for the shit I'm losing trying to clock her ass.* Chandelle played another forty-five minutes tallying her total for the night at forty-five thousand dollars. *Yes! I cleared fifteen grand in forty-five minutes playing conservatively. I can do this shit! Let me get the hell over to the cashiers' window and get my money and I'll be home free.* Chandelle walked from the high rollers room to the window and waited her turn to see the cashier. Ricky ducked out of sight as she passed and watched as she walked towards the cashier window. *She must've hit something. She ain't walking to the cashier if her ass was broke. I need to get out of here and get to Rena so I can find out what's up. Sorry Chandelle baby. It ain't personal but I gots to get mines and you're the means to do it.* Ricky waited until Chandelle was called to the window and turned in the opposite direction to leave the casino without being seen.

"How can I help you?" The cashier asked watching the clock noticing it was the end of her shift.

"I'd like to transfer my funds back to my checking account please." Chandelle handed over her casino players' card and her checking account number. The cashier took her card and swiped it into the casino waiting for her information to be retrieved by the system.

"Hmm, it must be getting late. The computer doesn't seem to recognize your card. Let me try it again." The cashier swiped the card a second time and again the system rejected her card as invalid.

143

"I'm so sorry about the wait Ms. Carter. Your card is reading invalid. Let me call a manager so we can get this issue resolved. Again, I am so sorry for the wait." Chandelle began to get nervous and tried to keep a straight face not to bring any attention to herself. *Oh Shit! Oh Shit! What should I do? I can't run because then I'll be guilty of fraud and definitely go to jail. If they notice something suspicious maybe I can just ask for the card back and tell them I'll come back tomorrow or something like that. I just gotta stay cool. I'll play it off like it's only twenty dollars or something like that so it won't seem like a big deal.* The manager came through the gate and walked towards the cashier asking her what the problem was. The cashier began explaining the circumstances while he began entering information into the computer periodically looking up and smiling at Chandelle. Chandelle nervously returned his smile as he continued typing away.

"I'm sorry about the delay Ms. Carter. It seems that your card is in pretty bad condition. You should consider coming back to the casino when the window reopens and exchanging it for a new one. They are free of charge and any cashier would be happy to help you." The manager again swiped the card and entered her account information. After being satisfied with the results he returned the card to Chandelle.

"Well, I have everything taken care of for you and you're ready to go. Again, I apologize for the wait."

"It's okay. Thank you for your help." Chandelle breathed a sigh of relief. She thought she was going to shit on herself as she pulled herself together to leave. The cashier passed the receipt through the window and logged off her computer to leave for the night.

"Your transfer is complete. Thank you for visiting the *Rivers Edge Casino*. Chandelle smiled and placed the receipt in her bag and headed towards the parking lot in a rush to get home to complete the transfer.

Chandelle was relieved she made it out the casino safely and felt secure that her plan went off without a hitch. But putting things in motion to include her friends was another story. She knew that execution had to be timely and flawless. *It took far too long to get this forty thousand. I need twenty times this much if I plan to move with a fresh start. I need to get the girls to the house tonight and hatch out a plan. I'm outta here by this weekend. Fuck the investigation, my job and tired ass Derek.*

Ricky opened the door to the apartment and noticed Rena lying across the couch sleeping. Quietly he climbed the steps to the bedroom to secure his stash under the floorboards. He pulled the money out the bag and counted out one hundred thousand dollars. *Damn! Tre was doing the damn thing! This motherfucker was robbing me blind! Then takes my money and flips it and moves me off the block. This hundred and whatever I get from Rena and Chandelle will be enough to get me the fuck outta here and dip from these charges.* Ricky bagged the money and headed down the steps to wake up Rena and find out what he needed to know to put his plan in action. Ricky stood over Rena and watched her sleep. *Rena is fine as hell. She definitely wifey material but shit happens.* Ricky thought to himself as he knelt down and planted a kiss on her forehead.

"Hey beautiful. Why are you down here on the couch instead of the bed upstairs?"

"Hi. When did you get in? I was waiting for you and fell asleep." Rena sat up on the couch and made room for Ricky to sit down beside her.

"I just got in a few minutes ago. I didn't want to bother you but you look so fine laying there I couldn't help coming over here and stealing a kiss."

"You're sweet baby. With everything that is going on I got nervous when it started getting late and you didn't make it back. Everything okay?"

"Yeah I'm straight. You can go on upstairs now. I'm in for the rest of the night. I want to watch some sports highlights then I'll be right up."

"No. I'll stick around with you for a little while. I'm waiting for Chandelle to call me. You know tonight is the night she was going out to the casino. She's supposed to call me and let me know that she's okay and everything went as planned."

"Oh yeah?" *Just said this bitch was wifey material and she sitting here running her mouth about her girl. She could never be my wife. She talks too fucking much! She'd have me in jail telling who the fuck knows all my business. Maybe I can find out what I need to know. This shit will be like taking candy from a baby.*

"Yeah, I'm just so scared for her. I mean Chandelle is smart as hell but this technology stuff can be traced. There's no telling if they can track her somehow or if they have something in place for people who try to rip them off."

"I hear you baby. You should be concerned. She's your best friend. So, explain to me again how she's doing this."

"Well I don't know all the details and I'm not sure I'd understand the whole thing if I did. But she has her casino card rigged so that she would be able to take the casinos cash without the casino knowing. All she has to do is take money from her checking account and put it on her casino card. But instead of the money depleting from her card it's doing the opposite and transferring from the casino to the casino card. She then will be able to take the money from her card and transfer it back into her checking account."

"Stop playin'! I don't understand that shit either. *So that's what the fuck she was doing! She was placing bets to transfer money onto the card. She can't lose! Then she went to the cashier's window and had the money moved to her bank account. I don't give a fuck how she was able to do it but I'm 'bout to get paid! I will just have to be patient and wait for her to walk to the window at the end of the night roll up on her then make her understand how she has to give up the cash if she wants to continue breathing.*

"How bout we go up to the bedroom and take the phone with us while you're waiting." Ricky licked his lips gesturing his need to have her and pulled Rena from the couch and led her to the steps. Before they climbed the stairs the phone rang.

"Hello?"

"Rena. It's me Chandelle. Girl, I did it! It worked Rena! I have forty-five thousand dollars!"

"Calm down! I'm so happy for you. I was worried to death all night. So, when are we going to do this?"

"That's why I'm calling. I had a couple of close calls but besides that I was thinking and I decided that we are going to move this up. We're going to do this tomorrow tonight."

"What? Tomorrow? Why so soon?"

"Just be here tomorrow morning and I'll explain everything to you then. Call Rachel and Nia and tell then to be at my house by nine-tomorrow morning. That should be early enough to put everything in place and be ready for tomorrow night."

"Okay. If you think we can do it the earlier the better. I'll call them now. I'll see you in the morning. Talk to you later." Rena hung up the phone and looked at Ricky who was waiting by the steps patiently.

"I guess you overheard. That was Chandelle on the phone. She wants me to call the girls. It's on for tomorrow. We have to meet her at her house in the morning."

"Alright baby. When you're done with all your calls meet me in the shower so we can pick up where we left off." Rena smiled and walked towards the couch. Looking over her shoulder she shouted towards the stairs,

"I'll be up in a minute baby. Don't use all the hot water."

Game For Fame

Chapter 21

Everyone was seated in the kitchen eating breakfast at Chandelles each eager to know the plan. Chandelle acted as the perfect hostess. She went out to the store at the crack of dawn to buy all the favorites the store had to offer. Her orders were for the girls to head straight for the kitchen where breakfast was being served buffet style. Bacon, eggs, pancakes, waffles, fruit and various juices and coffee were lined up across the buffet table. After breakfast and a full stomach Chandelle agreed to explain the plans for the evening.

An hour later after the dishes were cleared and put away the four women were drinking coffee and sitting around the dining room table.

"Well ladies, you have been under enough suspense. As you know from being here this morning, I was able to successfully pull off a trial run last night." Rachel was the first to speak up.

"I haven't had a chance to keep up with what's been going on lately. For the last week I've been comparing colleges trying to figure out which best suits my needs and how I can get into school for the fall semester. As you can guess, I can't afford to enroll on my income and loans are out the question because what I qualify for won't cover the full price of tuition. So, to keep a long story short, I'm in."

"I'm so glad you're going to be with us tonight. We need as much support for each other as we can get. Don't get me wrong. It's not as if we will be watched but because some of us will be able to get more money than others depending upon how we play, we can split up the money evenly at the end of the night. That will be more money for us to walk away with later."

"What do you mean Chandelle some of us will make out better than others? I'm probably the most in need right through here. I'm not trying to be greedy or anything but I'd like you all to consider my situation before we decide to make an even split." Rena stated.

"Oh no the hell you didn't! We all are taking the same amount of risk here. I sympathize with the fact that your mom is sick and you lost your job but I don't think I should give you more of my money because that broke down nigga of yours is trying to hustle you. Don't forget that my husband just left me with two kids to support and a part time job. I'm in just as much of a need as you are." Rachel said growing angrier as each minute passed.

"Calm down ladies! This is why I served breakfast first. We are best friends. Let's remember how much we love and respect each other before we start-arguing bout some money. We're better than that." Chandelle said trying to diffuse the situation.

"I agree with Chandelle. I'm already nervous about doing this in the first place. I don't need ya'll fighting with each other. Let's worry about how we're going to split it up after we get it. If you want to call it a worry." Rachel began laughing and they all joined in.

"Ladies did you all get your casino accounts set up?" They all nodded yes and Chandelle continued.

"Good. The next step is to go to the bank and have your accounts set up so that you can transfer money from your casino account to your checking account. Take notes and listen closely. You are going to take five hundred from your checking account to play with and then have any amount of money you have at the end of the night transferred from your casino account back into your checking account. When you enter the casino go to the cashier window tell then you want to set up a transfer account. You will give the cashier your ATM card, your checking account number and your casino card to make the transfer. Does everyone understand?" Again they nodded and took notes.

"Last night I started out at the dollar slot machines. Everything was fine but the money I was making was transferring at a slow rate." Chandelle was interrupted by Nia who stopped writing in mid sentence.

"What do you mean at a slow rate? You were making money weren't you?"

"Yes. But Nia I'm trying to make enough money that if I choose to work any time soon it's because I'm bored and looking for something to do. I'm not trying to be greedy but it took over an hour to pull five thousand out of the machine. I was able to get that in ten minutes playing the five dollar machines." Nia shook her head understanding her point.

"This is what I was thinking. I mentioned dividing our winnings later because one of us is going to play the dollar machines. I don't think it would be smart for all of us to be in the same area trying to steal from the casino. If something went wrong, and I don't expect it to, but if something went wrong one or two of us needs to be able to get away clear unnoticed. We're going to need that money for bail."

"Damn. I didn't even think about that Chandelle. Do you think that there is a possibility of being caught?" Rena asked.

"Nothing's fool proof Rena. But I already pulled this off and I have to admit that I was a little sloppy last night. I see you looking at me crazy Rachel. What happened was that I didn't get a new casino card. I used the old card I've had since the casino opened. Ordinarily it would be fine but because I had to add the strip on the back containing the program, when the cashier read it at the end of the night it didn't transfer the information as easily as it should have. I'm going to get a new card today while you ladies are tying up your loose ends. I'll need the three of you to give me your casino cards so that we can go to Electronics Depot and have the program attached to the back of the card. We are all going to go together to not arouse suspicion in case we need an explanation. I'll tell them that we are in an investment and to ensure our honesty we each will have a copy of our program to ensure we all will have an equal share in the profit if it sells."

"Damn girl you got this shit planned out don't you?" Nia asked impressed.

"I'm trying girl. Before we leave the next thing we are going to do is get on the computer and decide where you want to transfer your money. You cannot leave that amount of money in your checking accounts. Doesn't matter how much it is. But you been broke so you can't all of a sudden have anything over ten thousand sitting in your accounts because then you're going to have a problem with explaining it to the IRS. Now you girls said that you set up your checking accounts already and that's good but now you need an off shore account. I cashed out my 401k to start my off shore account. I know none of you are going to be able to do that because there isn't enough time. So what I'm going to do is give each of you ten thousand to open your accounts. I was able to take forty-five thousand from the casino last night and since we are all in this together I feel it's only fair that I share it with you." Rena began crying and immediately Chandelle began rubbing her back while Nia and Rachel looked on in awe.

"Chandelle this is the nicest thing anyone has ever done for me. I mean I was able to get a couple of thousand from Ricky when he was feeling generous but to do something like you're doing without any strings… I just don't know what to say. I love you girl." Nia and Rachel chimed in.

"Thank you Chandelle." Chandelle cut them off.

"You're welcome ladies. I love you all and we should have enough money to set us up comfortably for a long time. If we invest right and spend enough to keep us secure, I think we can take enough so that each of us can have five hundred to a million dollars each."

"You think that much Chandelle?" Rena asked wiping the tears from her eyes.

Y'vet

"I'm talking paid girl." Chandelle left the table and ran up the stairs to her bedroom to grab her laptop. She ran back down to the dining room table and directed her friends on how to open an offshore account. Ten thousand dollars was transferred to the Bank of Jamaica under each of their names. An hour later they were out the door headed towards the casino then Electronics Depot. They were to meet back at Chandelle's house at one to set out towards the casino.

Ricky waited at the house for a call by Rena. The night before he gave her the best sex she ever had in her life. His mission was to have her turned out and loyal for he knew what he needed to do in getting his hands on their money. As much as Rena ran her mouth he knew she wasn't stupid and she loved her friends especially Chandelle and was willing to do anything for them. His control was only going to be temporary and he had to keep her close as much as possible. Looking at the time on the wall mantle he noticed it was already twelve-thirty and she left the house at eight in the morning.

Where the fuck is she? She said she was going to find out what happened last night at the casino. I know Chandelle got out without a scratch because I saw her ass leave. Besides she called last night to telling her to meet at her house in the morning. I know she wouldn't go do the job without letting me know. Before Ricky could continue to grow impatient his cell phone rang with Rena's number showing up in the window.

"Hey baby. What's going on?" Ricky said cutting out the small talk.

"Good afternoon to you too. I'm with the girls and it's like I said to you last night. We're doing it today. I'm on my way to Electronics Depot to tie up some loose ends. I'll tell you about it tonight. We are going to the casino this afternoon and we'll be there till the cashiers' window closes at eleven tonight. So stay put till I get home tonight. I'll have your money and we can call it even."

"Okay baby. I'll be here for you tonight."

153

"Listen Ricky, I want to say something to you. These last couple of weeks has been crazy and to be truthful with you I thought that things were going to get ugly between us. But I have to admit that I really enjoyed you since you've been home. I wish that we could have been together and the circumstances were different. You're going to keep your promise and walk away without involving me in any drama right? I can't go to jail Ricky. I just can't." There was a pause on the other line.

"Yeah baby. You'll be straight. I'll see you when you get here." Ricky ended the call thinking to himself his next steps. *Damn Rena got me fucked up. I care about this girl and gonna miss the shit out of her. But a nigga like me can't carry no dead weight so I gotta get this cash. I'm gonna roll down to the casino get the money and head back here to pack my shit and leave town.*

Rena, Chandelle, Nia and Rachel stood in line in front of the cashier's window with five hundred dollars in hand.

"Ladies stay calm and let the cashier know that you are trying to open an account transfer from your casino account. Give them the five hundred dollars you are starting with so they can put it on your casino card. Then give them your debit card and account information from the bank so you can complete the transfer at the end of the night. When you're done meet me over at the first row of machines in front of the ladies room." Chandelle pointed towards the ladies room.

"Okay girls you ready? Rachel since you are the least experienced with the slots, you are going to play at the dollar machine. You will be the lookout and you'll be in a position to see all of us while the rest of are in blind spots and can't see each other or what's going on around us. You're the clear head out the group. Agree?" Rachel nodded yes and waited for Chandelle to finish.

"Rachel play the maximum bet. If you see anything that may cause you alarm, walk over to the high rollers room and let me know. We'll pack up and take what we have. Rena you're going to go with me at the

Waterside high rollers room and Nia you're going to be at the *Dockside* high rollers room. We will switch up between playing five dollar and ten dollar slots. Since we will be playing for close to nine hours we don't want to draw attention to the fact that we can afford to bet that kind of money. Periodically, we will walk out to use the restroom and get a bite to eat. Rachel you will be able to see all of us from your position at the dollar slot machine over there." Chandelle walked to the *Triple 7-dollar* machine she mapped out the evening before giving Rachel a clear view of her and her friends,

"This is where you'll play Rachel. You will be able to see us from here. If you see us get up to use the bathroom or go to the restaurant feel free to take a break. Does everyone understand her job? Any questions?" Rachel sat down at her machine and inserted her casino card and inserted twenty dollars and pushed the max bet button. Rena followed Chandelle to the *Waterside* and Nia headed to the *Dockside.*

Three hours later Chandelle accumulated a hundred and fifteen thousand dollars and Rena was doing equally as well. She gave Rena the sign to head towards the restaurant for a bite to eat. After finding a booth in the back and perusing the menu Rachel and Nia walked in the restaurant and took a seat at the booth smiling.

"I guess that I don't have to ask how well you are doing. By the looks on your faces the two of you are obviously doing very well."

"Hell yes! I have close to two hundred thousand dollars already and we have half the night to go." Nia stated excitedly.

"I have fifty thousand ladies. This is enough money to pay my tuition for school and have money left over."

"That's great girls. I have one hundred and fifty and Rena has one hundred. We are doing well. I'm going to hit the ten-dollar shots after lunch to increase our money. Stay calm like you been and we are home free."

"Chandelle, I'm not trying to bail out or anything but I think that maybe we should take what we have and come back tomorrow." Rachel said.

"Rachel this is it. I know it is tempting to walk out now but what we don't have enough to set us up for life. We would be able to pay our bills for a year or so and get ourselves out of debt but then we would be back to square one. I think it's riskier to try to come back tomorrow or any other day for that fact. I think that we should get what we can now and walk away without ever coming back."

"Come on Rachel. Don't back out now. We have been following Chandelle this far and she hasn't led us wrong yet. I say let's see this through." Rena said while Nia second it.

"I agree with Rena. I was asked for a divorce. I didn't want to bring it up before and it's none of your problem. I need this. I say follow the plan."

"I'm not getting scared. I just wanted to put it out there that's all. I'm with you. I'd never turn my back on you guys." Rachel said reassuring her friends of her loyalty.

"Okay since we all agree lets each lunch then get back to work. By the way, Nia I'm so sorry things aren't working out with your marriage. I just want you to know that I'm here for you but we have to stay focused. We're here for you."

After lunch the four of them returned to their machines except Chandelle sat down at a ten -dollar machine.

Three hours passed and Chandelle was close to having accrued a million dollars collectively. Thinking on her feet she made four trips around the casino hitting the various cashier windows in the casino and transferred money to her checking account to split up later with her friends. She couldn't wait to get home to make arrangements for her flight to the Bahamas that was leaving in the morning. Checking her casino card there was sixty thousand to add to her stash. She rose from her chair to signal her friends to head towards the cashier window so they could secure the money they already stole from the casino.

"Chandelle what's up? Why are we at the window now? We still have a couple of hours of gambling before we planned to leave?" Rena asked.

"I know. I have been getting up periodically securing some of my cash to my checking account. Remember, even though the cashiers don't know how much is being transferred at the end of the night we don't want to take any unnecessary risks trying to transfer a few million all at once. We have to hurry to a computer and transfer the money to our over seas accounts before our banks flag our checking accounts. By the time they see the amount in our accounts and raise any questions the money will already be gone." Chandelle said.

"You go girl! Your ass is on the ball thinking this shit out. I didn't even think of that. Why didn't you say something earlier? I could've transferred earlier than now." Nia stated.

"Because I didn't want any of you to get nervous or draw any unwanted attention towards yourselves running back and forth. I figured you cash in now and once more before we leave."

Rena, Chandelle, Rachel and Nia split up and stood in line at the various cashier windows around the casino and met back at the ladies room.

"Okay ladies what is the running total so far?" Chandelle asked.

"I transferred four hundred seventy-five thousand." Nia said proudly.

"Two hundred twenty thousand." Rachel stated.

"Seven hundred thousand." Rena said.

"Damn I thought I was doin' something. I have chump change compared to you Rena." Nia said laughing.

"Well, we are certainly doin the damn thing. I cashed in close to a million. I've been jumping around playing the ten and twenty-five dollar machines." The three ladies fell quiet instantly staring at Chandelle with their mouths hanging open. Laughing Chandelle said,

"Close your mouths. Ya'll look stupid as hell. I told you I was in this to retire. I'm not out here playing no games!" The four women began passing out high fives to each other.

"Okay get back to your machines and watch your back. We have two hours before we are home free." The ladies separated each going back to their machines.

Ricky walked in the casino looking for Rena and Chandelle. He spotted the crew hovered close to the bathroom and he immediately backed out of the aisle ensuring to keep undercover from being seen. Ricky watched as they dispersed and decided to keep an eye on Chandelle and follow her because sooner or later she would lead him to the money. His plan was to wait until she made the exchange at the cashier's window then follow her to make sure she understood that if she didn't withdraw the money and hand it over to him he would either kill her or exchange what he knew for a get out of jail free card on the charges being held over his head. *I really don't want to kill this bitch. But I will if she doesn't do what I want her to do. I don't think I'll have to worry about her because her ass is soft and I know she's not trying to take her friends down with her. However she wants to do this is fine with me.*

Ricky repositioned his gun in the waistband of his jeans securing himself that he was ready for whatever was about to go down. He sat down at a machine and placed a twenty in the bill holder pushing the play button keeping a close eye on his mark.

Chandelle decided that the extra two hundred thousand on her card along with what was already transferred was enough to make her life comfortable and didn't want to press her luck any farther than she already had. She pulled her card from the machine grabbed her purse and made her way to the cashier window to cash out. Turning around to seek out Rena she made eye contact indicating it was time to split up and cash out and meet at her house to tie up loose ends. Rena nodded in acknowledgement and signaled Nia and Rachel to head towards the windows towards the back of the casino to do the same. Chandelle stood third in line to be serviced when she was approached from behind.

"I guess you thought you would never hear from me again huh bitch? I've been watching your ass and you think you're slick. I been following you and I don't know exactly what you're up to and I don't care but you're a dead bitch."

"Angela? It can't be you. I saw your ass drive over the side of the highway and watched your car explode. You couldn't have survived that." Chandelle tried to turn around for assurance it was Angela and give herself space in case she needed to make some kind of move.

"Don't move bitch! I know you feel this gun in your back. If you move I'll shoot your ass right here."

"No you won't. You're in plain sight of all these witnesses. You wouldn't do something that damn dumb."

"Yes the fuck I will bitch. If I shoot your ass here, I'll convince the police it was self -defense because it was you trying to kill me by forcing me off the road. Your ass will be dead. What you going to do bitch? Tell your side of the story? I don't think so. If that don't work the worse they'll do is give me psychiatric treatment in some mental hospital for a few years. I can do that time standing on my head." Angela chuckled in Chandelle's ear.

"Now step out of line and walk towards the bathroom real slow." Chandelle stepped out of the line with Angela walking closely behind her.

"Listen bitch. We're going to use the side entrance and walk towards your car in the parking lot. If you yell or try to run I'm going to kill your ass. You understand?" Chandelle nodded yes and her eyes grew large as she saw Ricky approach Angela from behind.

"Hey Chandelle, how you doin?" Ricky positioned himself between the two and looked Angela up and down noticing how close she was standing to Chandelle.

"I'm fine Ricky. What are you doing here?" Chandelle was relieved seeing Ricky giving her time to come up with a plan but wondered if his timing was a coincidence. For the first time, Chandelle was able to get a good look at Angela. She still looked attractive in her jeans and t-shirt except for the scratch down the left side of her face.

"She said she fine nigga. Keep it movin and mind your own fucking business. We gotta go and you holding us up." Angela said stepping in front of Ricky trying to move Chandelle towards the hallway leading to the side exit.

" Who you talking to bitch? Chandelle is like my peeps. I'm tryna holla at her for a minute."

"Who the fuck you callin bitch mothafucka?" Angela turned and showed her gun hiding beneath the jacket draped over her wrist and pointed it at Ricky.

"Now keep it movin mothafucka before you get hurt." Angela pushed Chandelle closer to the exit.

"If you sportin a gun bitch be ready to use it." Ricky pulled his gun from his waist. Before Angela could react Ricky shot off a round landing in her chest. Angela hit the ground and the sound of the gunshot led everyone in the casino in chaos screaming and running towards the exits.

160

Chandelle looked around trying to spot her friends but didn't see any of them in hope that they cashed in and followed their plan.

"Don't try to run Chandelle. I want that money and I will shoot your ass if you don't hand it over." Ricky threatened. Angela slowly began to move and moaned in pain her hand inching towards her gun. Chandelle and Ricky looked down as Angela agonizing and wretching in pain drenched in a pool of her own blood. Ricky cocked back his gun to shoot her again when Chandelle dove to the floor reaching for Angela's gun. Ricky let go of a round landing a bullet in Angela's head while Chandelle grabbed the gun pointing it at Ricky.

"I swear to God Ricky I'll shoot you. Run while you still have a chance." Ricky looked around and noticed that the casino was nearly empty and heard the sirens of the police coming closer.

"I'll be back bitch. You can't hide and I know everything. Trust me you will pay or you'll be dead or in jail." Ricky ran down the hallway and out the door.

"Drop the gun! You're surrounded! It's the Pittsburgh Police. You're under arrest!

An hour later Chandelle was being held in the same room where she was questioned about the accident involving her and Angela.

"Ms. Carter. I must say that I'm surprised to see you here under these conditions." Chandelle remembered the officer as the first officer arriving on the scene of the accident out on the highway.

"Ms. Carter you are facing some serious charges. Murder in the first degree and weapons charges. You can wait for counsel but things will go much easier for you if you decide to cooperate now. I'm sure the DA will cut you a deal. What do you have to say for yourself Ms. Carter?" Chandelle watched as the officer paced back and forth and wondered if she should tell her side of the story. The only problem was that she didn't know exactly how much the police knew. Chandelle decided to let the police officer talk cause she figured he liked hearing his own voice and maybe she could get a idea on how much the police really knew.

Ms. Carter we are waiting for identification on the victim and it will only be a matter of time before we find out the motive. How was the victim related to you Ms. Carter?" Before the officer could get out another question the door opened and a familiar face entered the room. Officer Gaines looked at Chandelle then asked the interrogating officer to step outside.

Moments later officer Gaines walked in the room and took a seat across from Chandelle.

"Ms. Carter the victim in question was identified as Angela Washington. *The* Angela Washington that was engaged in the altercation with you out on the highway. The tapes released by the casino reveal that you were not the person who shot her but another individual not positively identified but suspected to be a Ricky Sheldon. I'd like to ask you a few questions if I may. Why didn't you say that it was Angela Washington in the casino with you when you were brought in? It would've saved you and us a lot of time. Second, are you willing to positively identify the shooter as Ricky Sheldon?"

"I'm just trying to protect myself officer. I thought maybe it would be better that I obtain counsel. But yes that was Angela Washington. She threatened to tell the police that I was the one harassing her and tried to run her off the road. I just hoped that the casino cameras would clear this up and obviously they did. I knew if I could get her on camera with her gun on me this horrible mess would be cleared up. Everyone would know that I wasn't lying and that she was harassing me and not the other way around. I hoped that she would just get sloppy but instead an altercation ensued between her and Ricky and well I guess you saw the rest."

"So the perpetrator was Ricky Sheldon? You will testify to that in court once he is apprehended?"

"Yes it was and I will testify to that in court."

"What caused Mr. Sheldon to take out his gun and shoot Ms Washington?"

"I think it was just the fact that Ms. Washington hurt his ego. She told him to fuck off for a lack of better words and I guess he just didn't appreciate being spoken to in those words. He dated my best friend. Well, she is more like my sister so I know of him. He always carried a gun from what I understand. So, he shot her."

"There are still some things I don't understand here Ms. Carter but we will need to find Mr. Sheldon to fill in the blanks. It just doesn't make sense as to why he was there and why he would shoot Ms. Washington in plain view of the cameras in a casino. For now we are going to let you go. But you will be needed for further questioning especially once we find Mr. Sheldon and bring him in. We'll be in contact."

I gotta get outta town before they catch up with Ricky. He can blow everything for me. I can't pay him because no matter what he will be wanted for killing Angela so paying him wouldn't solve any of my problems. I got to get home and get in touch with the girls.

Chapter 22

Chandelle opened the door to her house and turned on the lights startled by the sight of Rena sitting in the dark on the living room couch.

"Rena! I'm so glad to see you!" Chandelle ran to the couch and hugged her friend holding on for dear life. Looking into her eyes she and not feeling any response she asked,

"Rena what's the matter? Are you okay?"

"I should be asking you the same thing. I saw the police leading you out of the casino in handcuffs. I also saw Ricky leave right before you were arrested. Who was covered up on the gurney being led out by the coroner? When I saw Ricky running from the casino I was going to follow him but I stayed to find out who was shot. I heard the shots and started running with the rest of the crowd. I was so scared for you. I prayed it wasn't you and was relived when I saw that you were still alive. I didn't think you would be home tonight but I was going to sit and wait till I heard something."

"Catch your breath girl. It was Angela. That crazy bitch didn't die in the crash. Before I could find out how she made it out alive Ricky showed up and to make a long story short he ended up shooting her."

"Oh Chandelle! I'm so sorry. It's all my fault. I told Ricky about our plan to rob the casino. I didn't mean to betray your trust. I didn't mean for any of this to go down. I just wanted to reassure him that I was going to pay him his money. I didn't have any idea that he was going to follow you and try to rob you. I'm so sorry." Rena began crying uncontrollably.

"It's okay Rena. It turned out for the best. He got rid of my problem with Angela for me and now I don't have to worry about her anymore. The only problem I have now is getting out of town before the police catch up with Ricky and he tells them about the robbery."

"You don't have to worry about that Chandelle."

"What do you mean?

"After the police rode off with you I went back to my apartment after Ricky. Sure enough he was upstairs in our bedroom pulling back the floorboards. I asked him what he was doing at the casino because he was supposed to meet me at the house later on this evening. He told me he had his own plan and that you got what the fuck you had coming to you. I asked him what he was talking about and he said my stupid ass was the reason why you were going to spend the rest of your life in jail. He said I talk too fuckin much. Girl, I just lost it. Ricky's gun was on the bed so I grabbed it and shot him. I shot him Chandelle. I can't believe I done it but I just blacked the fuck out and pulled the trigger. When I was able to see what I'd done I grabbed the bag from the floorboards to see what he was after. Inside there was money and drugs. I took the money and put it in a bag and put half the drugs in the bag with it. I left half hoping the police will find it and say it was a drug deal gone bad."

"Damn Rena! We got to get you outta here. I got to admit though you were thinking. Where is the money from the casino?"

"I gave my card to Nia. They know you were arrested and they are scared Chandelle. I told them to go ahead with the transfer and I gave them access to my account to wire some money for me."

"I still have my card and I'm going to do the wire transfer tonight. How much did you get from Ricky?"

"I counted close to a hundred grand. I still have those drugs too. I don't know why I took them but I did." Chandelle smiled at her best friend and said,

"Well, we have enough money to start over. We can be on the next flight out of here. But it looks like we have some business to take care of first."

"What are you up to now Chandelle?" ©

Game For Fame

Made in the USA
San Bernardino, CA
30 September 2013